SUBLIMINAL

CARTOGRAPHY

A NOVEL

By Sean Leary

Dreaming World Books

This book is published in the United States by Dreaming World Books and distributed worldwide by Ingram, Amazon.com, Dreaming World Distribution and My Verona Productions.

The work is fictional. Any use of real names or details is speculative and in service of the fictional story and is not meant to be representative of factual events, nor should it be taken as such.

Very special thanks, as always, to my son, Jackson. Everything I do, I dedicate to you, my best friend and beautiful boy. I love you.

Special thanks as well to Matthew and Pam Clemens, for your incredible support, advice and friendship. I'll never forget it. Thanks as well to Dan O'Shea, Johanna Harris, Donna Pesavento, Gary Hudek, Frances Iskalis, and all of my family, friends, fans, and readers everywhere.

ISBN # (Print book) 978-1-948662-01-7

Library of Congress Catalog Card Number: Applied for

First edition print: 11-11-2020

Cover design and interior design by Sean Leary.

Website: www.seanleary.com. Email: seanleary@seanleary.com, and seanleary007@gmail.com.

For Jackson

INTRODUCTION

How do the decisions you make impact your life?

How have the paths you've walked, the people you've met, the choices you've made, put you on the journeys you've taken, and how has that connected you to others and your greater destiny?

Subliminal Cartography follows the winding and strange pathways of multiple generations of the Barstow family, and how a myriad of decisions led to the cascading effects of their lives. But has there been something more, something of which they aren't even aware, which has been guiding them, a lattice of coincidence and connection beyond their world and understanding?

It's all part of Subliminal Cartography, a beautifully-written novel leaping back and forth in time and space with a variety of colorful characters who have been united by one distinct symphony which connects us all.

Love.

This is one of my favorite books I've written.

I hope you enjoy the trip.

ONE

"I love you."

He looked into the face of his father.

Eyes clear and blue.

He held him like a child, like a baby, as his father had once done for him.

"I love you too."

His father had always been a night owl, which was a blessing for his mother when he was a baby. His father would wake up with him at odd times of the night and take him from the room, bring him into the sunroom looking out into the night, and hold this tiny, helpless being against his chest, against his heart.

He would feed him. Burp him. Hold him close and let him snuggle against the warmth of his chest, relax to the rhythmic beating of his heart. And his father would watch his most cherished son snuggled up against him and sing softly, or tell him stories, or read to him, the depth and calm of his voice nuzzling the boy to sleep.

"I love you."

When he got a little older, he would wake up with bad dreams or discomfort and his father would do the same thing. He'd wrap a big blanket around them and call it a nest, say he was the Daddy bird and he was snuggling up and protecting his baby bird.

"Tweet tweet," the little boy would say.

"Tweet tweet," his father would say, smiling.

The little boy, now a man, sat on the bed, holding his father as his father had once held him.

"Tweet Tweet," the son said, holding his father close and nuzzling his Dad's head against his chest so he could hear his son's heartbeat. The same heartbeat he'd once heard, so many years ago, as a wonderful, quick thwip on a sonogram, now heavy, slow, warm.

The father paused, and tears came to his eyes.

"Tweet tweet," the father said. "Love you baby bird."

"Love you, Daddy bird."

"Tweet tweet," his father said.

"Tweet tweet," he repeated, his little boy voice breaking.

He held his father's body close.

"Love you," the father said softly, "baby bird."

"Love you," the boy kissed his forehead, "Daddy bird."

"Love you, baby bird. Love you . . . son. Always."

The older man looked up into his son's eyes.

"Always."

And the father exhaled and faded in his arms, his eyes closed, a tear slowly moving down his cheek, down to a beautifully calm smile on his lips.

The boy held his father close.

"Love you, Daddy bird."

There was no answer.

"Tweet tweet."

There was no answer.

"Love you, Daddy bird."

There was no answer.

And then there was no sound, except the boy's slow sniffles that grew and grew into tremendous sobs and the sound of him crying, like he had when he was a child, in his father's arms.

TWO

His watery eyes broke open slowly, letting the black curtains part and the sleeves of light reach in.

He didn't know how long he'd been out. Wasn't sure if the images still dancing along the periphery of his sight were unconscious remains or retrievals he held to as long as he could.

Regardless, they faded. Sure, and silent. Faded. Gone.

His head pounding, he looked around the empty room.

It seemed to have gotten so much smaller than he remembered.

So much more silent.

So much more hollow.

The walls were marked with clean squares where the paint was still glossy, where pictures of smiles and happier times once hung. Now they were gone, all gone, leaving nothing but gray halos, dusty echoes of those buffers that halted the progress of the thin layer of decay that caked the house, invisible until now.

The baseball wallpaper and closet doors on the far wall still bore the faded traces of feverish crayon drawings, rising above an ocean of ragged carpet tarred and marred with errant day-glo drink stains, faded but seemingly impossible to remove.

At one point, the man had punished his son for dropping those drinks, for scrawling those marks.

Now he only wished there were more.

William Benjamin Barstow slumped, red-eyed and lumpy, melted into a corner of the room.

In the worn, shiny, brass doorknob of the closet across from him, he could see himself, small and warped.

Unshaven.

Unkempt.

Jeans unwashed. Shirt haphazardly buttoned. A haggard sportcoat. Ratty tennis shoes.

He looked around the room. Exhaled heavily and raised a gun to his head, first to his temple, then to the front of his head, then finally into his mouth.

He looked through the barren, shade-less windows and out into the verdant yard to a young evergreen tree. The sun beat behind it. Tears in his eyes, he remembered the day he planted it, with his son, so they could watch it grow, along with him, as the years went by.

He took the gun out of his mouth, shook his head, and dropped his hand, carefully unloading it and looking at the bullets, contemplating their failed trajectory.

A doorbell rang.

Ben continued looking at the bullets, closed them in his hand, looked around the room.

The doorbell rang again.

Ben rose, put the bullets into his jacket pocket, and tucked the unloaded gun into the back of his pants, beneath his jacket.

The doorbell rang again, just as Ben slung the door open.

"Oh, sorry!" The man outside awkwardly backed his hand off the buzzer, took a long look at Ben, and edged slightly backward.

"Oh, hey," Ben said, opening the door and jutting back into the hall.

"We're uh..."

"The Hannigans, right," Ben said, wearily. "Frank? Frank and, uh, Elise, Elise. Yeah, my, uh, my wife handled most of..."

"Yeah, uh," the man in the polo shirt and sweater smiled uncertainly, his wife following him with a nod and smile, as Frank gestured to the three others following them in. "Oh, uh, yeah, and um, these are our kids, or, well, at least our three oldest. Diana, she's, uh, fourteen, Melanie's thirteen and our son, Josh, just turned twelve."

"You have, four, though, right?"

"Five. The two youngest are with their aunt."

"Wow. Five. Must be a handful."

"Oh yeah."

"Wow, huh, hmm," Ben said. "Great. Um, yeah. I just, we, just have our son. Nick. He's, he just turned four. We haven't, uh, we didn't have any other kids."

"They're great," Frank said. "They're really, uh, excited about the move and everything."

The children examined the grizzled figure before them a bit uncomfortably. He looked kind of like they'd remembered seeing, when he'd say certain words or look a certain way, but only then.

"We didn't come at a bad time, did we? We had 11 o clock, right?" Frank said.

"Oh, yeah, it's, I, no," Ben said. "I guess time got away from me."

"We're not interrupting or anything? We can come back."

"Oh, no. I was just, uh," Ben put his hands into his jacket pockets and absentmindedly jangled the bullets softly, "contemplating some redecorating."

Frank and Elise nervously laughed.

"But I guess that'll be your call from now on," Ben said.

"Guess so," Elise said, smiling awkwardly.

"But that's not to say, I mean, we really do think the house looks great," Frank added. "I mean, you and your, I mean, you really, we think it's a really nice house. Well, obviously."

Ben took a deep breath and the room seemed to brighten just a bit.

"I think the kids and I are going to take a look around, honey," Elise said as the children took the cue to scramble.

"Oh, okay," Frank said, giving her a peck. "I'll catch up with you in a few."

She gave Ben a small nod of Midwestern politeness and moved past him, looking back and smiling, "We really love the house."

"And now you can make it a home," Ben said, with a smile and a sigh, as Elise nodded and moved on.

The two men stood silent for a few seconds as Ben looked at the door.

He pulled out a ring of keys from his pocket and handed them to Frank.

"Hopefully better than we did," he said, handing the keys over.

There was a pregnant pause.

"Sorry, sorry," Ben said. "I didn't..."

"No, no, we," Frank began, before stopping, waved off by Ben.

"I should probably go."

"Are you sure?" Frank stepped back as if opening the house back up to him. "You can..."

"No. I've said enough goodbyes," Ben said, opening the door. "It's not like anybody's answering."

The two men walked silently out the door, Ben's pace growing in strength slowly, surely as he moved down the path, trying not to linger too long, trying not to allow the memories to catch him before he got to the street.

They walked by a FOR SALE sign in the yard with a SOLD sticker on it.

Ben offhandedly pointed at it.

"You might want to..."

"Oh! Yeah." Frank took the sign out of the yard, bringing it with him, as he and Ben walked towards a sleek red sports car parked out front.

"Whoh! Nice ride! What is that, a '67?" Frank said.

"'66."

Ben looked it over, nostalgically, a slight smile crossing his face.

"I got this after my first big contract. Once the baby arrived it really wasn't practical. Rode it to and from work sometimes, but mostly it was just in storage," he said, shrugging. "She got the other car. The bigger one."

Ben sighed, exhaled heavily. "But, she also got our son. So..."

Frank nodded.

Ben quickly shifted, bounded back.

"I can't wait to drive it in winter. Should be a hell of an adventure."

Ben chuckled and gave a little wink. Frank smirked.

"You know," Frank said, smiling, "that sounds just like something you'd say. That...sarcastic humor we always used to like about you. You know, my wife and I, we used to watch you all the time. You were really good."

"Thanks."

Ben sighed.

"What?" Frank said. "I'm sorry, did I say something..."

"Nah, nah, nah." Ben looked down at the keys in his hand. "It's just... it's funny."

"What?"

"You never notice it," Ben said, "but compliments always sound better in the present tense."

"Oh, I didn't mean..."

Ben opened the trunk, pulled the gun out from behind him nonchalantly and threw it in among a bunch of clothes and junk – his remaining belongings. Frank jolted at the sight of the gun but pretended not to see it.

"Nah, I'm," Ben shut the trunk. "thanks for mentioning it."

Ben turned and put his hand out.

Frank shook it.

Ben looked back to the house, then to Frank, into his eyes, the slightest hint of a smile on his lips.

"Be good to her."

"Don't worry," Frank said, shaking Ben's hand reassuringly. "We've loved this house for a while. We were thrilled to get it."

Ben exhaled, took his hand away and smiled.

"No," Ben said, getting into the car. "I mean your wife."

Ben got in, turned the key and the car roared to life. With a final wave he bid farewell to the man with the sign, waving, standing in front of the house he watched fade, fade, fade over his shoulder and into the rear view mirror and then, over the horizon and gone.

Ben turned on the radio for a few seconds, flipped around to three stations and then turned it off abruptly.

The wind whipped over and around the metal cocoon as he gunned it onto the highway, faster, faster, faster, and then, he slowed.

He watched the exit signs pass.

Large and green, like cozy manicured lawns.

Signals.

Signs.

Directions.

To new destinations, to unknown places, to beginnings, to wide open spaces and chances to start again, start over, start anew.

His mind cleared.

The wind was a calm dull howl, a wave that washed his thoughts clean, a pristine plane.

With just one intrusion.

The sight of the two of them leaving.

The boy's last look.

Last tears.

Her hand on his shoulder.

"Don't worry," she said to the boy. "Everything's going to be alright."

Her voice broke.

But she never turned around.

For the first time.

She never turned around.

Ben sped up, burying the car into the red, ripping past trucks and cars, exits and stops, until the womb of white noise around him was deafening.

And then, he slowed.

Slowed.

Slowed.

He looked ahead to see the sign, like the haloed sigils in his son's room, yellow and glossy against the blurred, dirty horizon.

Slowed.

Slowed.

Looked ahead, to a sea of green exits on the right.

To a sharp gravely curve back on the left.

Slowed.

Slowed.

Then began to speed up.

Scanned the horizon, the earth and sky, closing in around him, and thought it seemed to have gotten so much smaller.

THREE

How do you die on a day you weren't supposed to live?

Alex had been booked for a business flight to New Zealand. He would've been propelling through the sky, smashing through time zones and the date line until he'd have lost an entire day of his life.

The day of his death.

Yesterday.

And now the only question was whether he had made the journey to someplace even more exotic.

Simon considered the paradox while trying to find a radio station without pig reports, earsplitting odes to the devil, weepy steel guitars or political mud-wrestling while losing seconds of his own life on the road through nowhere, Nebraska.

He'd had no luck.

His car, all 157, 286 miles of band-aids, baling wire and ``Beverly Hillbillies'' jalopy-style pure driving pleasure, had no satellite, phone connector, or even a CD player. The temperamental cassette player only worked when he wedged a book of matches into the player's mouth. And unfortunately, the machine was also viciously snotty about chewing up its cargo.

Simon was merely frustrated with its prickly, bitch rock critic nature when it devoured a Best of Stone Temple Pilots tape he'd picked up at a gas station.

But he vigorously protested its execution of Nirvana's "Nevermind."

He'd already learned a painful lesson after he'd punched the thing, one which still bled a little bit through the band aids he'd gotten at another of the many gas stations he'd hit on this trip. So, this time, as Kurt Cobain's voice turned into a murky, melting mess, Simon did the only thing any rational being dipped in the acid of hatred would do.

He pulled over, parked, removed the shoe from his left foot and used a ratty Chuck Taylor sneaker to pummel the dashboard diva until it released its victim, hot plastic oozing skeins of wrinkled brown magnetic tape.

Fine, thought Simon. See if I feed you again.

His plan to starve the beast was sorely tested by the lack of decent radio stations between cities, and his unpleasant alternative.

Without aural distraction he was left to rumination, rue and repeats of regrets he couldn't seem to shake, which lingered on, no matter how many miles were put between him and the place, and the person, he'd left behind.

And so, he thought over the object of his journey. The man who, in death, had somehow saved his life -- for the moment at least.

It was a strange way to return a favor, he thought.

New Zealand.

The contrails of a plane could be seen in the sky over him.

New Zealand.

They'd always talked about how cool it would be to go there when they were kids. And continued to talk about it as if it was a distant fantasy into their teens. At that point, they may as well have been talking about trekking to Mars. It seemed just as realistic.

Yet, by this point, Alex had been there enough times for it to have lost its novelty, and for Simon to become envious rather than thrilled by the postcards. It was yet another of Alex's globetrottings. He was never staying in one place for too long. It was just his nature. He figured one day he'd settle down, actually spend some time in one of the many houses and apartments he kept, maintained by his neighbors and the graciousness of friends.

Aside from being investments, the stray homes acted as a refuge for those souls to benefit from the free rent. They were an escape when needed to others. And the favors of those opportunities provided Alex with enough ersatz housekeepers and guardians to ensure the safety and integrity of the properties while he was gone, which was the vast majority of the time.

Simon had been one of those house-sitters. And as much as he resented himself for being in that position, even with his two current jobs, he lacked the independent funding to rectify that spot, at least not without making a significant move back to a far less expensive part of the country.

Alex's mother had been at her own house, also paid for by Alex, when Simon called.

``Hello?''

``Hi, it's Simon. Simon Barstow.''

``Thank you for calling me back, I'm sorry about the long message I left, but, I just wanted you to know, and, I don't know, I guess I just wanted to tell you, I didn't know if you knew,'' she said, leaving silence for a moment. ``I know you guys hadn't talked in a while...''

``No. No, but...''

``Everything was okay between you, right? He said you'd... everything was okay?''

``Yeah. Everything was okay. It was. Really.''

``That's good to know...'' she started to whimper a bit and had to pause to clear her head into a tissue. ``That's what he said. I never know, you know. I could never really tell. You know how it is, what you tell your parents is different than what you tell your friends. And you know, Alex was sometimes... you know.''

"Yeah."

Eventually he got the details from her, although the conversation was slow and intermittent.

He would've been preparing for a meeting, she said.

He would've been making plans for his vacation coming up after the trip.

He would've been brushing up on his language skills, hoping to assimilate during his next travels, to Japan and India, where he would've been even more of an alien.

29

Instead, he was being prepared for presentation, laid out for friends and family to see one last time.

And who knows where he had traveled now.

Simon wondered how long it had been since any of them had seen Alex. How many of them weren't sure if they would ever see him again? How strange that maybe this was the only way for him to be stopped, to be held in one spot, to allow them to realign with him, even if for one last time.

"What?"

There was a scritch of noise on the radio, surprising him, as a station leapt from the ether and, through static, began to come into focus. The words seemed distant, and then, slowly, stronger.

It was yet another talk radio show. This one criticizing the NASA efforts to send another lander to Mars, ridiculing anyone who might think there could be, or could have been, life there.

Simon remembered having this same conversation with Alex and their friends many times, from the time they were kids, up through their geeky, shared nerdfest of their teens.

"But what if we're landing in the wrong spots?" Alex said, at one point.

"What do you mean? That we keep landing in the desert and across the planet are booming cities?" Simon retorted.

"Wouldn't we be able to see that from observation? Even if we didn't land there, we've sent satellites around it and could see it from a distance.

"Yeah, but even that, that would only be from a distance, and that's only looking for what we expect to find, not keeping an open mind about it and reacting to what we discover," Alex said. "Maybe there's evidence there was life there, or maybe even still is, somehow, but we just haven't found it because we haven't sent enough landers up there and they haven't hit the right places? Or we're looking for what we think we should be looking for, instead of looking at what is and seeing it for what's actually there?"

Simon thought about it for a second. "That is true. I mean, think about if you were observing the earth and looking at the Amazon, or Antarctica, or the outback, and you couldn't see anything resembling life as you know it. Or imagine landing on earth from another planet. If you landed completely in the middle of the outback, you might think there's little to no life here. Or maybe hadn't been. Or in the Amazon, or the Arctic, you might find some life, but you wouldn't find humans."

"Yeah," Alex said. "And think about what you just said. Depending on where and when you land somewhere, you might make your entire impression of this planet, make your entire mind up, based upon just those one or two places you landed. You might think earth is all ice, or all desert, or all forest. Or even, think about it, you land in one spot during one season, and you think it's rainy or sunny or frigid, and that's just because of the vagaries of chance of you being introduced to it at that one specific time. I mean, you see it another time, and it's something else. And you go back and tell your scientists that it's one thing, and maybe another crew goes and experiences something entirely different, and the scientists are getting completely different data and trying to figure out what the truth is."

"But," Simon interjected, "the truth changes depending on the time you're visiting, and where, and all the other different factors. But it's still the truth, it's just a different truth for different people, or their perception of what the truth is at that time."

Alex took a long drink from a Mountain Dew.

"I wonder if this is what people talk about when they're high?" he laughed.

"Maybe it depends on the people," Simon shrugged. "Like landing on Mars. Some terrain is more hospitable to intelligent life than others."

Simon smiled remembering it.

And another late-night conversation, about whether or not people could be psychic, and if déjà vu was a manifestation of psychic power and we didn't know it.

And another, about whether we were currently living in a hologram or a computer simulation.

And another, about what their lives would be like ten or twenty years in the future.

There were so many. He and Alex had grown up just a few houses away from each other, and until Alex's parents split up and he moved across town, they saw each other every day. Thankfully, Alex's parents' divorce finally happened when the boys were 15, and it was just another year until they were 16, and able to drive, to hang out again. But the year had left a mark, pushed them in slightly different directions, and whatever they'd had just wasn't the same. Maybe it was because they weren't kids anymore. Maybe they'd crossed that threshold into the teen space where things evolve too quickly.

Landing on different parts of the planet. Navigation slightly off.

They were still friends, but the last year of high school didn't have the same bonhomie, especially once they discovered girls, and girlfriends began taking up more of their time. And then it was getting ready for college. And then it was college. And then they'd see each other on summer and winter breaks, in between working various jobs. And then it was life.

Alex had gone into computers, as he always said he would, and before long, he'd quickly skyrocketed to success, as he always said he would.

In the meantime, Simon toiled away, at a series of jobs that underpaid and under-stimulated him. Alex invited him to California, allowed him to stay rent-free in one of his apartments, a fun place near the beach that was filled with a rotating cast of wannabe actors and actresses, to give Simon the chance to catch a spark in some career, but regardless of where he landed, he didn't seem to find life.

They saw each other again at his sister's wedding, and there was too much to drink, and too many words said, and then too few words said, for a long time. Until finally, after hearing about George, and maybe that was the catalyst, it probably was, Alex reached out, and flew out to see Simon in California.

That was the best week of both of their lives since they were 14.

Two years ago.

The last time they saw each other in person.

Everything was great between them again, they'd call and write, but, life intervened, and Alex's job took him all over the world, and, as Simon had quickly learned, once you'd gotten away from the set structure of school semesters and summer and winter breaks, life became one long blur. Every day at work was pretty much the same with .0001 percent deviation from day to day, and it was all just a shrug and inertia from paycheck to paycheck. It was only in your personal life where there were any changes and milestones, and most of that had to do with any romantic relationships, and maybe that was why people his age were so interested in relationships, because that was the only real change and evolution and excitement and uncertainty left in their lives.

It was New Year's Eve, and you were kissing a beautiful woman, then it was March and you'd broken up, and then all of the sudden it was summer, and you're dating a girl you met at the Farmer's Market, then, before you knew it, it was August, and September, and, she's gone too, gone to graduate school to become someone new. And, so then you're moping through Halloween, drunk as hell, trying to pick up on a girl dressed up as a cat or tiger or something and failing miserably. And, then, holy shit is it really almost Thanksgiving? And what the fuck, how is it two weeks until Christmas? I need to get my shopping done. And then the next New Year, and you're drinking alone, and thinking of texting the one you were with the year before, and telling them how much you miss them, but you don't, and then you have some more drinks, and it's 4 a.m., and then you do, and then you forget and wake up the next day, and what's this message, and Jesus my head hurts, and ohhhhh man, did I really do that? Why did I do that? I said I was never going to text. And I didn't just, text, I called. Boy, not a good move. And, ahhhhh... forget it. It's done. And, no reply.

And then it's a new year already. And resolutions, and a new job, and going to a gym, and meeting someone else, and breaking up with someone else, and then repeat, and repeat again, and this looks promising, but then it isn't, and then you're like, why bother in the first place, and the gym membership becomes a monthly reminder on your bank statement that you haven't gone in a while, and man, I need to stop going out drinking so much with the guys from work just bitching about everything. And holy crap, the holidays are coming up AGAIN?

Jesus.

And, holy shit, you haven't seen your best friend in two years. The guy you've known since your parents met at a mall playground when you were both four, and started talking about preschools, and then they realized that they lived right down the road from each other, and how the hell did they miss that? And maybe it's just because we never really know what's all around us, what's inhabiting this strange world, all the time, until it finally, finally collides with our own lives, and takes on a meaning that it never did before, to either of us.

And... there goes the radio station again.

Out of range.

Stuck between stations.

Eyes back on the road he watched a pair of small cars, one red and one black, whisk by him in the other lane, passing by the metal whales in their path, the semis clogging the road. He wondered where the lithe vehicles were going; envied the impatience and carefree velocity of their drivers.

Simon snapped back in time to focus as he sped down the highway, about to pass a sign stuck alongside the road. The setting summer sun behind him flashed harsh on the shimmering green and white metal sheet and he had to slow down and squint to glean his location.

He was still so many miles away.

But he was in no hurry to get to where he was going.

His journey to the present slowed by the steady headwind of the past returning to him, welcomed like a warm summer breeze, because it was a far more pleasant place to be.

FOUR

I may be a girl.

I may only be 12.

Ok, almost 12.

But I still cannot fathom why a 13-year-old boy would think She-Hulk is the sexiest comic book character in history.

Nonetheless, that is what my older brother Simon's friend Alex is arguing right now.

Needless to say, I'm dumbfounded.

``She is!'' Alex maintains, waving a cheese fry in his hand for emphasis and amazingly not splattering any of us with its prefab gloop. ``I'm talkin' old school She-Hulk, like way old school. Before she joined the Fantastic Four and put on that stupid costume. Like, before, way back when She-Hulk first came out.''

``No way,'' Tark rolls his eyes.

``Seriously dude, think about it,'' Alex says. ``She's pretty much naked. When she used to go all Hulk and stuff, her clothes would rip off her and she'd only be wearing this seductively frayed shirt that would barely cover her. And then when she changed back to human form you could pretty much tell her boobs were about to fall out of the shirt. And her body was ultra-smack. It was really hot. Hot chick in barely there clothes? And she can kick major ass? You can't beat it.''

``Okay, points for almost nudity, but still, no way, man,'' my brother Simon says, taking a sip of his extra-large Mr. Pibb. ``For one thing, she's green. Don't you find that a little weird, that she looks like Marvin the Martian?''

``She's still hot.''

Simon leaned forward, incredulous. ``You mean to tell me she's hotter than any of the babes from Gen 13, hotter than Witchblade, hotter than Dark Phoenix or Storm or Emma Frost, or any of the Manga chicks, cripes, even hotter than friggin' Betty and Veronica?''

Betty and Veronica are Simon's picks. Both. Nice. T.M.I. Talk about a positive influence.

``Yes!'' Alex maintains, chomping into his fries with authority, as if the matter is closed by the force of his mandible.

``I still kinda like Sailor Moon,'' Tark adds out-of-the-blue.

``That's because you're a perv, Tark,'' I cut him off.

``Why does that make me a pervert?'' he says. ``C'mon, Faith, we go to a Catholic school. We've all gone to Catholic schools throughout our lives. Of course I'm gonna dig the uniform.''

``I guess. Perv. You're probably like one of those guys that draws fan art of her taking her clothes off and doing obscene things.''

``And what if I am?'' he laughed.

``Peeerrrrrvvv! Pervopolis! Pervy! Pervski!''

``Whatever.''

``Whatever yourself, Giorgios.''

``Don't call me Giorgios.''

``That's your name, freak.''

``You know I hate Giorgios. Call me Tark.''

``Why?''

``Just do it.''

``Okay, Nike.''

``Will you two shut the hell up?'' Simon interjected.

Giorgios, obviously, hated his name. But to me, Tark was even more stupid. Even if it was just shortening his last name, Tarkanian, so it made some sort of sense, but still -- lame.

At least when asked about their 2-D objects of lust none of them said Death from The Sandman comic. That's who I'm dressed as today. Darkness and whimsy in all her glory. She's been my fave for a while. To dress up as, to read about, pretty much all Death all the time for me. I just think she's cool. She's the best me I can think of -- supernatural powers added in, of course.

As for why I'm dressed in this way, as is typically the protocol in these situations -- comic book conventions -- we're all dressed as our favorite characters.

Tark is Rorschach from the Watchmen, although he took off his mask because it was bugging him and he only wears it for pictures. So basically, with his skinny face and big blue eyes and hawk nose and cowlick shock of black hair he looks like Inspector Gadget. And he hates it when we call him that.

Alex is Han Solo. Alex is always Han Solo. Except for the one time when I saw him as Fox Mulder from ``The X-Files,'' but that was at an ``X-Files'' convention. No, wait, sorry, Alex was Alex Krycek. Simon was Fox Mulder. I got to be Dana Scully, even though I don't look anything like her, other than the pale skin. I just had to wear a red wig. Then again, neither of those guys particularly looked like the people they were imitating either, aside from the costumes. Both of them look like surfers -- tan, tall, wiry, blond, blue-eyed -- although if either of them had a real muscle between them you wouldn't know it. Anyway, at this juncture, at this time, at this event, at this very moment, Simon is not Fox Mulder. He is Indiana Jones.

``I still think She-Hulk's the hottest,'' Alex said. ``You won't convince me otherwise.''

``Whatever, dude,'' is pretty much the consensus around the table.

Yes, these are my friends. And yes, we are at a comic book convention, eating in the cafeteria, waiting to get the signatures of Jeremy Bulloch and Peter Mayhew, better known as the actors who played Boba Fett and Chewbacca, respectively. And yes, we are complete and utter geeks. And yes, we don't care what you think and we're quite happy with it.

These are our lives. These are our loves. We're not harming anyone and we're having a good time. Get over it.

From the time we were young we were into this stuff. Blame it on our older brother Nick, who eventually gave it up for girls and sports, much to our chagrin. But once he introduced me and Simon to comic books, sci-fi, role playing games and the sort, we were hooked. And so were Simon's friends.

When we were younger, Simon, Tark (then known as Giorgios) and Alex used to fashion crude capes from our parents' curtains, wrap them about themselves and tear around the neighborhood, throwing mulberries at cats, knocking over garbage cans and doing various other things that caused their parents to get irate phone calls.

Grounding didn't work. Threats didn't work. So, for some reason, the logic of which still escapes me, they assigned Simon to act as my babysitter, taking me everywhere he went, thinking that would cramp his style. Instead, it turned me into a tomboy geek.

I'd never really fit in with my friends at school. At almost six feet by the time I hit 11, I was looked on as an Amazon, some mutant from the missile test range. And don't think my oh-so-sensitive classmates didn't remind me of it at every opportunity. My railroad track of braces and the gigantic glasses clumped over my pasty face didn't help. They only made me look a little like Kareem Abdul-Jabbar, a likeness which I was only too happy no one else in my class had noticed. Nothing against Kareem, but that's a nickname I could live without. That's why I also stayed away from basketball. Just in case.

The comic book world afforded me something of an escape. A girl my size was looked upon in its domain as a force to be reckoned with. And with every story I read about a female warrior or superhero, my self-esteem grew. If they could be cool, so could I.

Not to mention that hanging around with guys like this didn't make me feel like such a social pariah. In the world of sci-fi, any girl of remote attractiveness, especially one with a lanky body like me, with long dark hair who could pass for Goth, was considered a goddess.

As time went on, I think my brother realized this, which is one of the reasons why he kept me around. It gave his group a sort of cache to have a girl within their ranks. Even if the girl was his sister. Those looking in from the outside didn't need to know that bit of information. And besides, if there was one girl in the group, maybe the other girls at the event would feel more comfortable allowing my brother and his friends to approach them. It was a logical theory, and it couldn't hurt. The lot of them had never had anything approaching a date, unless you count partnering up for science projects.

None of them had mastered that mixture of cruelty and indifference that proved intoxicating to junior high and early high school girls. They remained clueless and overeager, squandering attention even in the rare instances they attracted it, obliviously boring to death even their co-ed pool party companions -- who, themselves, were invariably fellow nerds -- with long monologues on videogames, the symbolism of

``Battlestar Galactica'' and the subtle nuances of the universe of X-Men comics.

My parents couldn't understand it. Things were far simpler in their younger years, and even when they were raising Nick, who was around five years before either Simon or I were born. It didn't seem like much of a stretch, but in kid years, and trend years, it was huge. Nick had come along before any of this had gone anywhere close to mainstream, and was raised accordingly, spending most of his time outside playing sports and getting into trouble in ways that made my father smile and remember the things he did when he was young. When Nick was a kid, videogames may as well have been played on an abacus, for how primitive they were.

For Simon and I, it was much different. There was no curfew at the street lights, there was us being home long before dark. The world had seemingly become far more dangerous, and so, it was a lot more time inside, and given the far wider array of options, everything from cable to videogames to this strange new thing called the Internet, we didn't mind.

However, my parents, and especially my grandparents, may they rest in peace, were concerned. Maybe it was too many stories in the media about the corrupting influence of things the writers didn't understand, maybe it was just them trying to make sense of things they didn't understand, but there was more of a hovering around me and Simon, subtle nudges, however well meaning, to help us fit in more.

As if that was ever going to happen.

I still remember the one time I overheard my Grandmother asking Nick, with concern in her voice, if Simon was gay.

``Well, I just never see him with girls,'' she said. ``He never brings girls home and he spends so much time in his room with his friends, playing those Dungeons and Dragons games. Do you think they're into weird things in those games and that's why they're called Dungeons?''

``He's not gay, Grandma,'' Nick said, stifling a laugh. ``He's a geek. There's a big difference.''

``What do you mean?''

``Well, let's put it this way,'' Nick said, ``if he was gay, he'd be avoiding girls. Because he's a geek, the girls avoid him.''

``Oh,'' she said, pausing for a moment to let it sink in. ``Poor Simon.''

``Don't worry, he'll be fine,'' Nick said. ``It might not be until he gets to college, but he'll be fine. He just needs to be in a place where people understand him.''

Indeed.

These gatherings were necessary to our mental health because they were the only places we really fit in with the rest of the untouchables.

The theory of like molecules gravitating inevitably toward one another was proven true with us. Slowly, through repeated treks to comics and record shops, conventions, Dungeons and Dragons nights at the local library and video game emporiums, we began to coagulate into something of a clique of our own, however leper-like our colony may have been considered. But, bonding over our shared misery, we became each others' friends and thankfully discovered we had more in common than our outsider status. We all enjoyed the insular world of reading and the fantastic realms of science-fiction and fantasy. Not a surprise at any stretch. When the real world is intolerable, imagining yourself in anything else is not only a pleasant departure but a prerequisite to survival.

Even if what you imagine yourself to be is an elf magic user with an absurdly high number of hit points.

Within a few months we had developed a web of like beings to communicate with. Strangelings of various ages and developmental deformities from a smattering of schools within our area.

But even within that group, there were still levels of status.

``Hey Faith, there's your boyfriend,'' Tark elbowed me, pointing to the back of the cafeteria and chuckling.

``Shut up, Giorgios.'' I punched his arm.

Schlepping to a table at the far end, carrying a tray full of food, was a kid one might generously describe as portly.

Okay, he was fat, there was no way around it.

But you had to admire his guts.

Okay, bad choice of word. You had to admire his courage.

Because this guy, all probably two-hundred pounds of him, was crammed into an exact replica red-white-and-blue Captain America outfit. Complete with winged mask and round shield slung behind his ample torso like a backpack, to allow him to carry his food.

And on top of it all, rather than the blond haired, blue eyed Aryan Steve Rogers (the secret identity of Cap in the comic books), this gent was Hispanic.

``Didn't you say you thought Captain America was the sexiest?'' Tark said. ``There ya go.''

I did. I did say he was the sexiest. And he was, to me, at least. Sure, there were cooler characters. Wolverine, for one. Batman. Sandman. Even the Silver Surfer. But there was something cool about Captain America to me, about the whole idea of him. About a guy who was so pure in his motives, so determined, that he wound up getting himself literally frozen in time, back in the '40s, back in this era of innocence, before being thawed out and reborn again at a later date. An adult who still had that idealism. An adult who still had that fight. It was very appealing to me.

``There's your luuuvaaah!'' Tark laughed.

``Yeah, and there's yours,'' I said, pointing to a tall, muscular man dressed as an even more dominatrix-like version of Dr. Frank N. Furter from ``Rocky Horror Picture Show.'' Frank sidled up to the condiment bar, grabbing relish packets and stuffing them in the straps of his black leather panties while making an obnoxious show of spraying mustard over a large hot dog on his tray. He and his companion, a stout woman dressed as Magenta, made obscene gestures and laughed.

``Keep that mental picture for later, Tark, I know you want both of them.''

The other guys cracked up as Tark stewed.

I looked back at the good Captain as he laid his tray down on the table and poked through a bag he'd had hanging over his arm. Pulling out a sketchpad and a few pencils, he began to draw with his left hand as he slowly, carefully lifted a greasy pizza slice up to his mouth with the right, taking a huge bite.

He let out a deep breath and his torso heaved, the blue spandex of his costume shining in the sun coming in from the picture windows on one side of the café. Ahhh. Smiling, obviously relaxed, pizza in one hand, pencil in another, what looked to be a gigantic plastic bag of comics on the table down from his tray, he seemed perfectly content and happy in this land where even he could be seemingly immune from torture.

And for a second, I admit, I kinda fell in love with him.

``Aren't you gonna go sit with him?'' Tark laughed.

``I just might,'' I snapped. ``It's better than sitting with you.''

``Cut it out, Tark,'' Simon jumped in.

``Yeah, don't be a dick,'' Alex said. ``That guy's in the same boat as us. He's here at the convention to get away from getting busted on every day. Give the guy a break. Do you want us to start calling you Log Nose here, like everyone else did at Eisenhower?''

``Screw you, Alex,'' Tark said, his head dropping down towards the table. ``Or should I say, `Basket' Case?''

``Leave it alone,'' Simon said. ``Let's just be happy we're away from that crap and enjoy the day and let others enjoy it too.''

``Fair enough,'' Alex said, pausing, before adding. ``But I still think She-Hulk is the sexiest.''

We all laughed.

Three minutes into a conversation about whether or not Ghost Rider was all flames and a skeleton under his suit, or whether there was some kind of body there, I noticed that our live-and-let live outlook hadn't spread to everyone in the cafe.

Sure enough, it didn't take long for the law of the jungle to be enforced even among the runts of the pack. A trio of guys dressed like Stormtroopers and a Darth Vader descended upon Captain America like an Empirical rain cloud, no doubt hurtling insults his way from the look of it.

When Darth's first punch smacked upon the Captain's ample upper arm, the flesh jiggled ferociously. You could hear the laughter all the way over on our side of the café when he struck it again, harder, as the Captain kept his face down, looking at his food, obviously hoping that if he ignored them, they would go away.

``Poor dude,'' Simon said.

``Someone should do something,'' Alex added. ``Where the heck is security?''

I looked around. Security was apparently out to lunch like the rest of us. I glanced at the three guys stuck at our table, like the dozens of others in the café pretending not to notice, hoping not to be noticed, not to find themselves as targets. Then I looked back at the onslaught. The hyenas had already started to pick things off the Captain's plate and the Stormtroopers were doffing helmets to eat their stolen Ding Dongs and Ho Hos.

There was nobody around to do anything. There obviously was no security. The workers behind the counter either couldn't see because they were too busy, or couldn't be bothered because they weren't being paid enough to be. And as for the rest of the crowd? Well, let's just say geeks aren't all that good at confrontation.

But I couldn't help myself. Sure, at school I would remain stoic as the insults rained down, holding it in, pushing down my pain until I got home, to the safety of my room, where I could finally cry and let it all out. Finally release all that hurt. Punch my pillows and whale on the punching bag I had in my room and then when I was good and worn out, lay back on my bed, listening to music and reading whatever comics I had left, unopened, from that week.

But here, for some reason, I felt empowered. Maybe it was all the admiring glances I had gotten throughout the day. Maybe it was a soft spot for Captain America. Maybe it was something more. Like the fact that I was probably a good six inches taller than all the guys who were picking on the good Captain. But I couldn't stand by and watch this occur.

``You guys really are a bunch of pussies," I said to my companions, standing up and beginning to stride with purpose towards the table of misery, leaving my brother and his friends behind.

My stomach leapt around in my chest like the monster in ``Alien." My hands sweated streams. My throat stuck and parched. But I kept going. And all the while, all I could keep on thinking was, ``What the heck am I going to say? What line or catch phrase or something could I use to get them to stop, and then if they don't, what am I going to do?" At the very least, I was hoping that if they started in on me, someone would come to my defense. Someone who at least maybe wanted to score points with a girl, even if I was the girl. I hoped.

"Hey, leave him alone!" I barked, my voice cracking.

They all turned at once, helmets at their sides, revealing acne scarred faces, sweaty, greasy hair and cruel, jagged teeth. There was a pregnant silence in the cafeteria.

"Yeah, and what if we don't?" Darth Vader finally spoke up. "What are you gonna do about it, huh?"

He stepped forward and his hands shot into my chest. He actually pushed me. Or he was trying to cop a feel. Probably a little of both, although there wasn't much to cop.

"Huh?" he said, as the Stormtroopers cackled. "Huh?"

"Stop, or what?" he pushed me again. "Or what?"

"Or this, dickhead!" The sound came from behind me, as did the plate of cheese fries, smacking Darth in his red pitted face. With a berserker scream, Alex slammed headfirst into the pile, knocking Darth backward into two of the Stormtroopers and sending all of them careening to the cement floor.

I turned around just in time to see my brother's Mr. Pibb whipping in midair, glancing the remaining Stormtrooper in the shoulder. My brother always did have terrible aim. But you just don't mess with Mr. Pibb.

At this point, as if on a director's cue, all hell broke loose and the masses began piling up on Darth and his henchmen, food sailing everywhere, costumed characters crashing into each other and sending one another slipping to the floor. Bits of colored plexiglass and cardboard and plastic cracked at the force of their falls, and the wails of despair over the carefully-crafted outfits meeting their doom filled the hall.

Once the melee broke out, it didn't take long for the cafeteria workers and security to finally take notice and break it up -- more likely than not because they wanted to stop the mess they would have to clean up before it got too out of hand. Darth Vader and his pals tried to blame it on my brother and our crew, but, emboldened by their success, the crowd sided with us and all fingers were pointed in the way of the Empire.

The security guards led them out, each of them crying at the defeat and, even more so, at the shabby state of their uniforms. Parents would undeniably be called and punishments would be meted out. Justice would be served. Superman would've been proud. Especially since a tall, redheaded kid dressed as Superman had also joined in by getting a good stride on, throwing a half-eaten peanut-butter sandwich and biffing a stormtrooper in the head.

And at the table, Captain America shined, free again.

``That's the first time anyone's ever stood up for me," he said, practically near tears.

We all looked at one another.

"I think that's the first time we've ever stood up for each other," I said.

Foodless at this point, we all sat down at the table as the Captain shared what was left of his feast with us. We looked at his drawings, which were pretty good, mostly pictures of a lone hero fighting his way diligently through a large mass of foes, sending bodies sailing with powerful punches and kicks.

His name was Hector and he went to Louisa, a school in the town next to ours. He had loved Captain America since he was a kid, in part because he was the earliest superhero he had encountered. His grandmother, who had been the first of his family to make the trip to this country, gave him the comics when he was just learning to read, enthralled by the red-white-and-blue logo. She was the one who had made him the costume, and although he realized it was ill-fitting on him, whenever he went to a convention he knew it would disappoint her if he didn't wear it.

Typically, he was immune to abuse since most of the people around him were of a heavier set. But there were a few times he was hounded, and those would lead to a sabbatical. Not just from the costume, but from the conventions themselves.

``I like the costume," I said. "That's a really cool story."

He swelled with pride.

We spent the rest of the day with Hector. We waited in line for autographs, saw a few sneak previews of comic book films coming out the following summer, checked out some panel discussions with artists and spent plenty of time on artists' row and among the boxes and boxes and boxes of back issues, debating the finer points of our pet galaxies and stepping to the fore to defend our fantastical passions.

At the end of the day, as we were walking through the halls of the convention center, on our way to the parking lot, we saw a familiar sight. The Empire crew. From the looks of things, they were still waiting for their parents. It was not good.

Hanging around near the doors, with a thick-armed, tattooed security guy with a graying beard and reddish ponytail keeping an eye on them, they were a sad, withered cadre. With most of their costumes torn away, they reminded me of Daleks -- emaciated and pitifully vulnerable without their ominous exoskeletons. Concave chests, insect arms and waists that looked minuscule compared to the huge, padded costumes still sheathing their legs.

They shot us glances of fear mingled with anger and disgust. When one of them mouthed some sort of insult and ``scratched his head" with an upturned middle finger, Alex gritted his teeth, pretended to cock his fist and fake lunged in their direction. It made them flinch, and Alex laughed. But once his fist was safely out of range, with a second to compose themselves, they whipped up even more poisonous vibes our way.

Hector and I, bringing up the rear of our group, got the most withering stares.

Looking back quickly to make sure the security guy couldn't see, the jerk pretending to be Darth made a quick but unmistakable oinking sound in Hector's direction.

But I didn't let it matter.

The second I heard the sound, the moment I saw Hector start to deflate, noticed his step grow just a fraction heavier, I did the one thing I knew would be guaranteed to raise his spirits and completely demolish theirs.

I reached out and grabbed Hector's hand.

Grasping it back, shocked, he looked back at me, and I gave him a quick peck on the cheek.

Blushing, his huge smile caused his chubby cheeks to burst beyond the constraints of his costume's cowl, sending the wings on the side of his headgear upward at an odd angle. His stride perked up. He was a superhero again.

We looked at each other, matching grins. His paw snugly holding mine, we strolled out the doors, a couple of misfits, unfrozen, reborn.

FIVE

"Oops...almost got it."

The little boy scrambled to retrieve the football wobbling on the floor, the footies in his blue flannel pajamas skittering on the carpet. Reaching around the rough, leather oval, he shotputted it across the room.

"Good throw, Aaron," the man said, catching it. The almost-three-year-old smiled widely. Nick underhand tossed it, and just as he had taught him, Aaron brought his small arms together to cushion the ball's downward slope, then clutched it, struggling, to his chest. This time it did not drop.

"Good throw, Daddy," the boy beamed, reflecting the pride shone upon him. He stepped back with verve and launched a pass unexpectedly high and fast.

Nick leaned and fell to grab it before it went beyond them. Like the boy, he made a special effort to snag every wobbly throw. The loose closet door behind Nick was closed, but the broken doorknob would offer little resistance to solid impact, and the packed boxes piled behind it were full of questions best left unopened.

Nick's eyes scanned the clock as he rose. Almost two hours beyond bedtime. He felt a twinge of guilt. He promised himself only 15 more minutes.

But Aaron was far from tired. It almost seemed as if he could tell, but how could he? They tried to hide it as best they could. But he probably felt; in the hugs lasting longer than usual, the moments more filled, the words carefully considered.

In the other room, his mother was soundly asleep. This would not be her last night with the boy.

However, Nick knew there would be no more like this —- for any of them. And so he savored every detail, trying to fit an infinite picture of his boy into a too-small space. Trying to insure he'd never forget a gesture, a sound.

He'd clap his hands when he laughed hard, especially when the mice tripped over each other in "Shrek." Sometimes he walked on his "tippy-toes," particularly if he had a cookie in his hand. Certain words he said were still slightly unformed, like "peese" and "duice."

The boy's biological father, the woman's ex-husband, had left a week after the boy was born and was never heard from again. Upon returning home from the hospital after having Aaron, the woman placed the baby's medical bracelet in an antique box with her wedding ring.

Nick met them a few months later. They moved in with him a few months after that.

Nick remembered her asking, when they first met, if he could ever love this child as much as his own flesh and blood. With no frame of reference, he could say nothing but an optimistic yes.

Now he wondered if he would ever love any child as much as this boy.

As the ball floated between them, Nick rewound the last two-and-a-half years in his mind; trying to find signs, symptoms, something he could point to. When the crack began to form. Instead he found evidence he shouldn't have ignored, and countless memories of the one reason he chose to overlook it. Ironic, that as her business trips grew longer, her calls less frequent, he seemed to relish more and more her time away, time left between the two "men of the house." Friday nights spent reading Dr. Seuss. Saturdays going to the park. Pushing grocery carts, making racing car sounds. "One and a highchair, please."

Dusk being met by two darkening figures; a small one being pushed on a swing, the other reciting a letter of the alphabet with each nudge.

Nick never imagined that somewhere else, two darkening figures would be greeting the night in a far less innocent fashion.

They hadn't been married. There was only talk that dwindled in intensity as the months flipped by, replaced, Nick thought, by a sense of security greater than ceremony. He trusted. Never suspected. Now he wondered how long it would be before he could ever be that trusting again.

"Daddy?"

Nick had held the ball in his hands too long. The boy rushed him, giggling, jumping on him and yelling. The man laughed, dropping the ball as the boy tried tickling him with small sausage fingers.

"Keep it down, buddy, Mommy's trying to sleep."

Nick held one arm around the boy, giving him little noogies on his head with the other.

"What's your name?"

"Aaron."

"How do you spell your name?"

"A-R-N."

"Noooo...A-A-R-O-N."

"No, A-R-N."

Aaron wiggled as Nick patted his head.

"We need to get a brush through there pal, you've got knots in your hair."

"No, Daddy, knots not in hair. Squirrels eat knots!"

The man chuckled, as he had the first time the boy said it.

"That's right, and you know, if you don't brush your hair, you might get hair-squirrels."

"I not get hair-squirrels."

"You just might. They're very rare, but they have been seen in these parts, and they can be quite tricky. They could zoom in and hide in your hair and you wouldn't even know it, until they started to build their nests in your ears. In fact, I think I see one...right...there!"

Nick jiggled a finger behind the boy's ear, throwing him into fits of laughter.

"Right...there!"

"Daaaaady! Stop!"

"OK," Nick hugged Aaron and kissed the top of his head. "I think I got 'em all out."

Aaron put his hand in his hair. "There no hair-squirrels, Daddy."

Nick sighed. He shifted the conversation topic to bedtime, as much as he dreaded it.

He knew that when Aaron left in the morning, he wouldn't be picking him up that evening, or any one afterward. That night, Aaron would be driven to a new life, and Nick wondered how long it would be before Aaron understood that he wouldn't be going home. Or at least not to his home. The only one he'd really known.

The two walked to the bathroom to wash up, then headed back to Aaron's room. Nick tucked him in. He kissed and hugged him goodnight, twice, brushed the hair from the boy's forehead and kissed him again, trying to hold his tears.

Aaron looked up at him sadly. He could tell.

"I snuggle you?" Aaron held out his arms. "Snuggle you, Daddy?"

"OK, buddy." Nick laid down and Aaron rested his head on the man's chest. For a long time, there was silence.

"A-A-R-O-N," the boy whispered, and they both drifted to sleep.

The next day when the man woke, the boxes, and the boy, were gone. There was a quick note, about when she would be back to collect the rest. By then the man would be at work, seeking distraction, activity. Anything but contemplation.

Two weeks later, the last phone call was made when she knew he wouldn't be home. Aaron was having a hard time, and she felt it best if there was finally a clean break. No more phone calls. No more visits. No more confusion over whether Aaron should call him "Daddy" or "Nick" when he told stories to the other kids in daycare.

Nick listened to the message seven times before finally erasing it, along with any thoughts of struggle. He loved the boy too much.

He found his pistol, loaded it, considered its weight in his hand.

When he returned it to its place, the handle was warm, the nose cold.

He sat in the boy's room. It smelled like an infant. Baby powder, ointment, stray candy, spills. He looked around at the bright starred wallpaper he pasted two years earlier.

His heart dropped. His pen followed. He began to write, stopping only to stretch, allowing himself to fall into it as deeply as possible, knowing that it would be that last time he could afford to do so for quite a while. Motion would replace feeling, blur it, to enable him to heal. The pictures he had tried so hard to capture would have to fade.

Five hours later he would go to a post office and place a thick envelope in a metal box that would remain as static, as steadfast, as the fidelity expressed inside.

And he imagined, fifteen years later, a boy with an old football on a shelf in his room, receiving an unexpected package for his eighteenth birthday. He would open it to find a key and a brief note.

On the Friday before he'd leave for college he would drive half a day to the city where he was born. On marbled steps, Aaron would read from a yellowed envelope.

"When I first saw you, you were asleep. A beautiful, gentle boy with chubby cheeks that bobbed with your incredibly loud snores. They made me smile, and when I leaned over to brush a hair aside your forehead, the hall light framed your face and left me a mental picture I would carry with me forever. A portrait of my little boy. My 'porkpie.'

"This is everything I remember about you. Everything you were, and always will be, to me, and everything I hope you still are to yourself..."

SIX

The rug the Pope puked and pissed on lies on my porch, cleaned of everything but the memories.

Of course, its defiler wasn't the Pope then; he was only my roommate.

I was awakened with news of his promotion early on Martin Luther King Day. Too early. Mistri. She was the only one who would dare to call before noon on a day off.

"Lambchop! What are you doing?"

"I was holding a full house and had Jennifer Aniston down to a Wonder Bra."

"Riiiiight."

"Can this wait? It's MLK. A holiday? I'd like to get back to sleep so I too could have a dream."

"Simon Barstow! It's 1 p.m.!"

"And?"

"You should not be sleeping."

"I was dreaming. There's a difference. One is merely utilitarian. The other is creating an alternate reality, and the portal to another dimension, another life, a gateway."

"Whatever. You are so full of it."

"Okay. I'm not going to argue. Why are you calling me?"

"Did you see `Reformation' last night?"

"I'm going back to dreamworld."

"I'm going to keep calling you."

"I'm going to turn off the phone."

"I'm going to come over and knock on your door."

"Is that a code phrase for something sexual?"

"If it is, you probably don't want to know it."

"I don't know, I'm pretty adventurous."

"Yeah. Right. No comment there. So, did you see it?"

Forget it. She's hopeless. Especially when she wants to talk bad TV.

"Reformation" was one of our new favorites, a cross between "One Life to Live," "Goodfellas" and "The DaVinci Code." The church hated it, but viewers loved it. After all, where else could you see a trio of ninja nuns, who looked like "Charlie's Angels," vacationing in Ibiza, while clandestinely on the prowl for the Spear of Destiny?

"No, I recorded it," I yawned.

"Dude, you're not gonna believe this. Moochie is the new Pope."

"Huh?"

"Moochie. Michael Mancuso. Your college roommate, my ex-whatever, is the new Pope on `Reformation.'"

"You're kidding."

"No! A man we've both seen naked is now the most powerful man in the church. Well, the fake church anyway. Still, do you think that makes us sinners or something?"

"You, maybe. I never slept with him."

"As far as you can remember."

She was joking, but in the unfocused kaleidoscope of that drugged, drunken, debauched time, who really knew for sure?

The first words Moochie said to me, the inaugural day of freshman orientation, as he walked into our antiseptic dorm room, were, "So, you wanna get high, or what?"

For the next two years of our lives, there was plenty of getting high and "or what." He was a drama major. I was a graphic design major. A vast portion of our hazy days was spent "suffering for our art." This incredible sacrifice included recycling beer cans, selling plasma and soaking our parents (hence, "Moochie") to buy cheap booze and drugs.

That enabled us to conduct "chemistry experiments," which was a creative euphemism for parties throwing random chemicals of beings (or should that be chemicals and beings?) together to see what would explode. Invariably, this would ultimately lead to one or both of us enticing likewise melodramatic and broken female art and drama majors into affairs that would give us all a rich well of existential grist for our budding masterworks. And, also, plenty of orgasms.

Both of us thought we were going to be incredibly famous someday. Everyone does when he or she is 19. Especially in Southern California. In our demented little heads, where gray cells struggled in vain against a thickening horde of inebriates constantly attacking them, we were slowly assembling our back stories to the legends we would become.

So, when Moochie drunkenly urinated on himself and the floor as several goth girls fell down laughing, somehow prompting him to croon "Waterloo" by ABBA, it was chalked up to a "Keith Richards moment" rather than simple drunken incontinence.

Mistri, so named because her parents were big fans of Agatha Christie, and, also, marijuana, was sucked into our black hole sophomore year, just after that first of many infamous rug incidents. She lived across the hall. Moochie met her late one night, while shambling to the drinking fountain, wearing only his boxers. He was looking to fill a bucket for the waterslide we had built in our room, using duct tape, pillows and Hefty garbage bags. Two co-eds whose names I cannot remember but whose skimpy bras and panties are indelibly etched in my mind, were eagerly awaiting their turns on our homemade Wacky Waters set.

Aside from Moochie's quest for agua prompting his departure, he also wanted to find a place to potentially vomit that wouldn't leave our room stinking any worse than it already did. False alarm, but I think he was impressed that Mistri stood around waiting even as he dry-heaved over the fountain. It turned out she was just bored and curious as to whether or not he was going to go through with it.

"Is there some reason you're not wearing pants?" Mistri chuckled.

"They were too tight," Moochie smirked. "I couldn't figure out whether it was because of my large wallet or my extra-large penis."

"It's probably because your ass is getting fat," she sneered, pushing him out of the way to get to the fountain before he actually did emit something rank into it.

The next day, we became better acquainted with her in the cafeteria during dinner/breakfast. She was looking for distractions and adventures, which were our specialty.

By fall break, we had incorporated that sweet, strawberry-blonde haired nymphette into those adventures. Soon our disease had also spread to her friends, the recovering private school girls with whom she filled life by alternately emulating and living vicariously through Sylvia Plath, Jewel, and the cast of "Melrose Place." Good times.

Judging from the fuzzy memories and my squiggled journal entries, it was a gripping ride while it lasted. But before long, things began to sour. Grades sagged, sycophants and succubae flunked out, and, inevitably, boredom and inertia wedged Moochie, Mistri and me into a hellish love triangle.

Its surly unraveling led to a summer incommunicado between the three of us, and when junior year cracked open, Moochie was gone. Apparently, he mis-delivered two dozen pizzas to a friend's party, called his boss, Leonardi, to tell him to fuck off, grabbed a backpack and hopped a bus to Hollywood.

At first, Mistri and I gathered sordid tales from mutual friends he kept in touch with, but eventually we both got postcards, then letters, more or less making amends and in a warped way, thanking us.

"It was a call," he wrote, at the end of a long missive kvetching about dead-end auditions, roach-swarmed apartments shared with psychotic strangers, and jobs wearing giant foam foodstuff costumes. "It was a crossroads in our lives. The kind of drama we'd been pursuing all along. And it ended up happening when we least expected or wanted it. She chose you, and for a while I hated you for it. But failure MUST breed opportunity to move forward. I needed to completely disengage to fulfill my destiny."

Part of me thought he was right. The other part wondered if he had joined a cult or had been watching too many episodes of "Oprah."

But he really had changed. He kept at it, pursuing his acting career through hundreds of auditions, hundreds of rejections and countless meals of ramen and hoarded condiments. And after we'd made our peace, throughout the trek, he kept in touch. Maybe it was only to remind him of what drove him there in the first place. Maybe it was to rub it in that while we were settling into typical lives he was still living the exotic. But he kept in touch. Even up through his first commercial, as a skateboarder extremely enthusiastic about a new orange drink, we had a subscription to the colorful "Moochie newsletter."

However, as his imdb database entry fattened, eventually our subscription expired. Christmas cards were returned to sender unopened, old phone numbers were discovered to be disconnected and Moochie became a fond flashback; worth a smile when he would pop up as an "expert scientist" on an infomercial or as a hit-and-run victim on a medical drama.

Mistri and I took the paths most taken, and it made all the difference. I got into advertising, and moved into an apartment generously sublet from my friend Alex, who's never in town. She works in one of those nebulous business jobs I can never quite remember the specifics of, but which I know has some resemblance to all the Dilbert strips taped up around her apartment.

We remained friends, occasionally hooking up during dry seasons in the romance department, but spending most of our time trying to fool ourselves into thinking we're vibrant characters in a romantic comedy of our own making. It enlivens and distracts us, although sometimes not quite as much as the evening soap operas we use to get through the more brutally banal stretches.

MLK morning, we chatted and fast-forwarded through our respective tapes of Moochie's big debut, as the "hip, young, new Pope who may just know the true resting place of the Holy Grail," according to TV Guide.

We decided to meet at La Flama Casa that night for cheap, strong Margaritas and enchiladas with an inevitable side order of regrets and self-examination. Once there we slipped into our familiar roles as drunk and drunker, with her verbalizing parallels to what I was thinking but hadn't imbibed enough to express. Vibrant images of coulda, woulda, shoulda beens that we secretly hoped were taking place for us in some alternate reality with such vitality that shockwaves would spread from them, ripple throughout our many alternate lives to this one, and slowly, but inexorably, draw us nearer to our manifest destiny.

Segueing out of a story about a tragic prom date that had been told with subtle variations close to three dozen times, she told me about an old phone message she pretended to have just found, but which I guessed she had been cherishing among high school pictures and love letters for quite a while. It was from a few years ago, during the time Moochie was a regular correspondent.

When we got back to her place, she played it for me, fast forwarding beyond other messages she'd had saved, including a diatribe from another ex-boyfriend begging to get her back and a few strange but amusing blips from her nerdy brother. Just past a "Happy Birthday" call from her three-year-old niece was that familiar, dusty voice.

"Hi, uh, yeah, this is Mike Mancuso," he chuckled, "I just found this number in my jacket. I was wondering if you were by any chance the lawyer I talked to about helping me get custody of my fifteen Cuban foster children from my ex-boyfriend Tom Cruise?" Laugh. Click.

"You know, we could probably get some bucks from `A Current Affair' for that tape," Mistri slurred, smiling.

Hours later, after a brief, awkward exchange of bodily fluids and a boring, repetitive exchange of insecurities and doubts afterwards, Mistri passed out and I left, hoping I wouldn't be too hung over for work Tuesday.

In the light of a full moon, errant bugs that seemed to be casually flying nowhere smashed against my windshield. It was like driving on the highway during the tail end of a snowstorm.

When I got home, I opened up the front closet to hang up my jacket, and looked down to see a rusty easel and my tool box brimmed with ancient, squeezed up paints and frizzed brushes. I closed the door.

Looking down, I walked out the front door again, onto the porch, into the night, and stopped. Looked out over the quiet neighborhood, listened to the city bustling with activity just out of sight. I stood there for a few moments, on the cheap, ugly rug drabbed by footprints and time that covered the floor just outside my doorway. It was well past its prime, and should've logically and reasonably been thrown out long ago, but I'd had it since college, and it was still red and vital in reminiscences.

I remembered feeling awful for Moochie that junior year, but also jubilant, having Mistri to myself, even by default. It seemed terrible for him at the time, I'm sure. But it turned out we did help him, by giving him no reason to stay.

And now, perhaps he was returning the favor, in a way. Maybe his success was my own "call," as he put it -- something to smack me in the ass like a rolled, wet towel, to wake me up from my taupe, IKEAed existence. Maybe this was the turning point, to show me what I could've done, should've done, with my life. Perhaps this was the seed that would bloom with me walking away from my job and pursuing something trendy, cool and entrepreneurial. Something that felt substantial. Whatever that was supposed to mean.

Or maybe it was just a trivial brush with fame, several times removed, which I could use at a party, to spin into a conversation on the vagaries of luck and chance.

Screw it. I could ponder and stew tomorrow, while I was on company time, pretending to be thinking about something else.

It was late. My alarm would be blaring before I knew it, prodding me into another clock-punching day. And my comfortable bed was calling my name, promising me another night of Jennifer Aniston and a good hand.

SEVEN

One last slash, and a red streak stained the white expanse, oozing and dripping into a pool as the two sides split harsh and complete.

The man jolted at the sight and dropped the knife onto the counter, unsettled for a moment. The crimson droplets clinging lightly to the metal blade exploded from it as it hit, and he could feel them splatter like shrapnel against his bare arm, causing him to flinch.

A cry broke his attention and the sight of little legs moving caused him to regain his composure and wipe the sweat from his forehead.

A small voice from below him.

"Daddy?"

Smaller.

"Daddy?"

He took a deep breath.

Turned to his son, watched him slowly kicking the pedals of his tiny red tricycle, sneaking towards his father, smiling as he ambled across the kitchen floor.

"Are the orangies done, Daddy?"

"Yeah, yeah, buddy, they're all done."

The man ran the knife under hot water and watched the remaining blood orange juice disappear down the drain. Put the knife back safely out of reach of inexperienced hands. Ran a towel under the faucet and wiped clean the counter.

Or at least attempted.

"Shoot."

He rubbed harder. Still, the slight marks remained.

"Aaah, shoot."

"What Daddy?"

"Nothing, buddy, nothing."

He put the towel aside.

The man carried the plate of thin orange slices from the kitchen along with another plate of small sandwiches and chips into the dining room. His son pedaled herky-jerky to keep up.

"Want to sit here?" the man asked, as the boy nodded.

Hector held the plates safely aloft, as the boy climbed off his vehicle and into a chair next to a second, larger one, both of them at a table by the window, looking out into the garden. While the man set their places the boy flipped through a pile of mail on the edge of the table.

"Daddy, who's Hec-tor?"

"That's Daddy, buddy."

"Hec-tor is Daddy? I thought your name was Daddy? Your name is Hec-tor Daddy?"

"It's both, Luis. It's like you – your name is Luis but I call you buddy."

"Oh, yeah."

"People can be more than one name, but they're the same person."

The boy shrugged his shoulders and nodded.

With Luis settled in, Hector put his thick arm around him and kissed the top of his head, then started eating, gingerly helping the boy when needed.

"MC," the boy said, looking at the man's tattoo.

"Yup, buddy, MC."

He knew the other letters, his father had taught them to him, but regardless of repetition, for whatever reason, the boy would never say them. Always the same two. MC. The father found it curious, but never minded. The tattoo was from a former life. One far from the smiling, chirping toddler who made up his new one.

They ate quickly, looking out on the bright of the day, each looking forward to basking in it. When they were through they cleaned up and were out the door, on their daily walk, hand in hand, down the street, past the regular yards, which never failed to entertain the boy with their simple charms.

"Reptar!"

The boy grasped the man's hand tighter as the small, skinny, dog lashed across the fenced-in yard, ripping up grass and earth in its claws and launching itself, jaws bared and barking, at the chain link fence.

The fence gave slightly with each futile attack, but held, and ultimately rested once they'd passed by and the dog had lost attention to move on to a passing squirrel.

"Why does Reptar do that?"

"Because that's what he's been taught. He thinks he's protecting his yard."

"But we weren't going to take anything," the little boy said.

"I know buddy."

"But he was biting the fence."

"Yeah."

"Did he want to bite us?"

"Well, maybe he's afraid of us."

"Why would he be afraid of us? We were just walking by saying hi to him. We walk by his yard all the time. And he has a fence."

"I don't know, buddy."

"Why was he being mean?"

"I don't know," the man said. "Sometimes that's just the way things are."

"But sometimes he doesn't do that, sometimes he just lays on his porch."

"I don't know, buddy."

The boy looked confused for a few moments, but it passed once the church was in sight.

Behind them, a man jogged lightly and the dog slathered and yelled and slammed against the fence again, before fading to a hollow bark.

"Now he's barking at that man jogging!" Luis said.

"See," Hector added, "he always does that to everybody, not just us. That means it really doesn't have anything to do with us, it's just the way he is, the way he's been taught."

For a second, with the whine of the dog in the air, Hector halted and it was back, back for him.

The air. The night. The last night. The staccato bursts of orange and red and white crackling the dark. The soft thwap and the spider webs of blood, blood and body clutched in his hands as he fell into the dirt, again and again, into the dirt, trying to get up, failing, failing, until he just stayed down. Down. Hearing the sounds of men. The sounds of the orange and white and red flashes and the thud of others going down to the dirt. The cries. The sounds of distant dogs. The dogs. And the silence. And the sound of the men crunching carefully around him, their voices alien, cold, then drifting, drifting away, into silence, the only sound the dogs. Then as the dark gave way the thwap, thwap, thwap of metal carving air in the gloam of the pre-dawn, the fog, and that rotor caressing the air above him, aside him, as he was lifted up, away, the last sound, the dogs, distant and afraid.

The world was savage and dirty and teeming and bleeding fire.

And then it was cold and white and caged in artificial light.

And then, he was home.

He was home.

And for the first time, he saw him.

Saw his boy.

Saw his wife.

Blood and body.

She cried when she saw him again, for the first time.

When she saw his leg.

Saw his arm.

Saw his face.

Cried for him.

Cried for his pain.

But cried in joy.

Knowing that pain had bought his life.

He wouldn't be going back.

He wouldn't be leaving them again.

"Daddy, there aren't any cars coming."

His son held his hand tight and they crossed into a parking lot opening up to a building with a giant cross spread out before them, like arms gathering them in.

Walked past it to a playground, uninhabited by children at this time of the day.

He held his son's hand as he climbed along precipitous paths, nudged and pushed him as he yelled "Higher! Higher!" on the swings, stood beside the slide and the tires, ready to catch his boy if necessary.

The tire swing moved back and forth, and his son's laughter ebbed and waned as it swung.

His son was a pendulum, passing between Hector and the sun, dark, then light, dark, then light, dark, then light.

Dark, then light.

Dark, then light.

He remembered the wait.

The wait for the light.

The wait.

As they crept from the darkness, slowly, cautiously, seeping over the carnage they'd wrought, scavenging what they could.

Kicking the dead, prodding the corpses.

Just to be sure.

Jarring the shells of men left behind.

Talking, laughing, just hours before.

Now silent, as other men, soldiers like them, were walking about, talking, laughing.

Walking around the bodies.

Silent.

All but him.

All but him.

The only one breathing, seeping blood, panting, praying, alive, just barely.

Waiting.

Waiting.

For someone to find him, or find him out.

As the men with the guns and the bayonets and the alien sounds and voices closed around him.

And he saw.

He'd only told two people.

What he saw.

As he waited for the last shots, the last thrust of metal into him, the final beat of his heart, he kept repeating the same images over and over, the same images he wanted to be his last.

His wife.

His child.

And then, he saw.

Over him.

Around him.

Saving him. Somehow. Somehow, he remained alive, somehow, was overlooked by the soldiers looking to kill any survivors.

Hector had seen.

Something.

That saved him.

A bright light.

A hallucination.

Brought about by shock, by trauma.

That's what the doctor called it.

The doctor had walked out, looking at Hector sadly, softly, the same way the nurses did after the doctor whispered to them, told them.

His wife saw it as something else.

He'd been asleep at the time, she said.

Asleep.

Away.

A silent beacon.

Bringing a wayward ship home.

Safe.

They were walking back when he saw something out of the side of his vision, advancing on his boy, quickly, and in a split second he turned to smack it down, with such force and speed it startled his son.

"Daddy! What did you do?"

"I thought it was a bee, buddy."

"What is it?"

They walked tentatively to a dark spot on the dirt road home.

"Stand back, buddy, I'll step on it."

"No, wait!"

They looked down.

Saw the struggling, pathetic thing with its bent leg and wing, scratching in a circle.

"It's not a bee."

"It's a grasshopper."

"Why did you hit it like that? You hurt it."

"I thought it was a bee, buddy. I thought it was gonna hurt you."

"You thought it was gonna hurt me?"

"Yeah."

"And you were protecting me?"

"Yeah."

The boy examined it.

"Is it gonna die?"

"I don't know buddy."

The boy looked around at the birds sailing nonchalantly overhead.

"I think he might get eaten."

The man moved over towards the bug, shifting his foot closer, closer, until lifting it slightly.

"Do you want me to?" the man said.

"To pick him up?" the boy said.

The man put his foot back down, away from the bug, and looked at his son, looked at his face, into his eyes.

The boy smiled, but his forehead remained wrinkled and sad as he looked down at the bug, which had gone still but for a subtle twitch that showed it was playing dead.

"Can we save it?" the boy asked.

"Sure, buddy."

The boy directed his father to stand by the bug, to divert any potential traffic down the road from it. Then, with utmost care, he took a large, green leaf and scooped the bug onto it, cupping it into one hand and lightly arching his other hand over it. The grasshopper struggled a bit at first but then gave in and allowed the boy to carry it home, where he and his father fashioned a small house made of a mason jar, holes poked in the top, populated with the grasshopper and some chopped grass and leaves "for food."

Later, when his mother came home from work, her son greeted her, running into her long, pale arms, as her husband walked slowly behind, a slight limp, smiling, kissing her and wrapping her tall, thin form up in his huge grasp.

They walked into the house and she marveled and oohed and aahed over the flowers they'd picked for her, kissed and hugged the man and boy, and acted similarly impressed at their new housemate, which had seemed to stir to life in his confinement, the near-constant conversation of his young companion a seeming panacea to the day's harried events.

Later that night, they sat on the porch and watched as the sun slunk over the horizon, inking the trees and turning the skies to aqua and purple and orange, watched the first few fireflies flicker over the lawn and the boy, carrying the jar, talking to his new friend, introducing him to his fellow bugs he'd, assumedly, never met.

The man laughed, shook his head.

Proud.

"That's your son," he said to his wife.

She looked at the boy, talking to the bug in the jar.

Looked at the man.

"He's your son too."

The man watched the boy for a second, surrounded by light, a life bourn in his hands.

"Yeah," the man said. "He is."

EIGHT

"We'll be fine," Nick replied to the question unasked, but implied by the odd look in Marisol's eyes. "You go ahead, we'll meet you later."

The call had come at the onset of "family day." The one time a week when work was banned, housework was shrugged off and everything aside their unit of three was ignored.

Usually.

Today, like many other family days, was being spent at Rootin' Tootin' Rocky's Fun Time Place, where you could be a kid, no matter what your age. It was pretty much Aaron's favorite place in the world, and by extension, it was one of theirs, because they loved to see him so happy.

They were halfway into lunch when her cell phone rang, dipping her into awkward euphemisms at the table and finally taking her to hushed conversation away from it.

"Julie," she said, putting her finger over the phone mic before she moved away, and really that was all that needed to be said.

"Julie," Aaron imitated, with a shush, and laughed.

"So, what should we do now?" Nick said to the boy, crossing his eyes and making a face as Aaron bubbled up in laughter again.

It was a while before she returned to the table. In the meantime, with his Mom away, Aaron and Nick had made the most of the situation. They polished off the lukewarm pizza and played a game they called "werewolf fangs," where the craggy, discarded crusts were placed just under their upper lips to simulate the game's namesake. Although in Aaron's case, most often the crusts were hanging precariously from his mouth, it hardly mattered. The sole object seemed to be Nick acting like a complete goofball to make him laugh.

Lycanthropic possibilities exhausted, the duo headed for the gaming area. Nick looked around, but no sign of Marisol, so he changed out a five to arm himself with quarters for a forklift booth bursting with stuffed animals.

``Get the bike, Daddy! Get the bike!'' Aaron nodded his unruly blond head over his red-and-white striped sailor polo and placed his pudgy paws on the game's counter, next to the joystick.

``I'll give it a try, buddy. Daddy's not the greatest in the world at this game.''

Three dollars and a dozen attempts in, Marisol returned from outside, harried, lightly sweating, her pale skin flushed dark pink and the ends of her auburn hair stained dark and frizzy.

"Sorry, Nick, you know how she is."

``What's up?'' Nick said, never breaking his gaze from the metallic arm.

She shook her head and exhaled, exasperated, opening her mouth to speak and then stopping, as if she didn't know what to say. As she stepped closer, Aaron scrunched his nose. She smelled like an ashtray.

``I thought you'd quit?'' Nick said, pushing the button on the joystick. The metal arm gently grabbed ahold of the toy they'd been seeking and finally took hold, lifting it from the morass of plush.

``Yaaaaaay!'' Aaron burst out, watching the clamp loosely lofting the red plush motorbike to drop over the exit square on the machine.

``I know,'' she said. ``I did. I will. I know it's not good for him. I've just been under a lot of stress lately. Work, everything, and the whole Julie situation has just been driving me nuts.''

``Don't worry, the trip will do us good,'' Nick said, smiling at her and then fishing the toy out of the game's slot and handing it to Aaron, who immediately ran to their table to play with it.

``Yeah,'' she sighed.

After the fun palace, they were set to hit the mall, to the Travel Agency, to make the latest payment on their vacation. A trip for three to Mexico. Aaron's first extended trek away from town. Nick's first extended time away with Marisol since they'd started dating two years ago.

The initial plan was that it was going to be just the two of them. But when two family babysitters -- one being the aforementioned Julie -- proved to be unavailable, they succumbed to the wheels of fate and started planning on taking Aaron along. He didn't quite grasp what they were doing, and it needed some explaining to him, but once he latched onto the idea of them going to the country where tacos were invented, he found it to be very exciting.

``So what's up?'' Nick said, as he and Marisol watched the boy from a safe distance.

``Oh, the usual,'' she said, looking down at her feet and scraping the bottom of her sole against the tile floor. ``She's, uhhh . . . things aren't going well again.''

``Issues with Tom.''

``Yeah.''

``That sucks.''

She looked up. ``Do you mind if I go over there?''

``No, I guess not,'' Nick said. ``We'll miss you. We haven't seen you much lately.''

``I know. I'll make it up to you. When everything is okay with Julie. Alright?''

``That's fine. I understand. I'm just worried about the little guy.''

``I know,'' she trailed off, looking at him. ``He enjoys being with you though. You guys have a good time together.''

``Yeah,'' Nick said. ``Don't worry about us. We'll be okay.''

And they would be. They always were. Especially over the last few months, as they became more of a duo than a trio. But Nick couldn't be too angry. Julie was rarely okay lately, from what he could tell. Since late spring, Marisol and her once-estranged sister had been nearly inseparable. Late nights, after work, weekends, the calls would constantly arrive. Always on the cell, always with some frantic reason for Marisol to leave them behind.

Nick was kept out of the loop for the most part. From what Marisol said, and from the uncomfortable vibe he got from Julie when he gently offered any help he could, he got the feeling she didn't feel steady with many people knowing what was happening. That was fine with him, he could respect her privacy.

Still, he started to feel odd about it a few weeks ago. Some things just weren't adding up. Details, things mentioned in Julie's presence, things mentioned by Julie, that seemed incongruous with previous events, spurred him to ask Marisol if she was being completely honest.

About a month back, at the end of what began as a potentially dangerous talk, Marisol, after swearing him to silence, told him about the abuse. And everything changed. Suspicions and accusations turned into guilt and a willingness on his part to do what needed to be done.

If this meant more time solo with Aaron, so be it. Not that Nick minded. Quite the contrary. But he did feel bad for her, missing out on what had been a quicksilver formative time for the toddler, an era of new words and phrases, new foods and games, first rhymes and songs.

At the table again, she put her hand on Aaron's back and kissed him on the top of the head.

``I'll be back before dinner. Reservation is at six, right?''

``Yeah,'' Nick said. ``Just meet us there. Tell Julie she's welcome, and to bring the kids too if she wants.''

``Sure,'' she said, looking at Nick with wide eyes that grew glassy for just a second. ``I'll see you later.''

She leaned over and gave Nick a quick peck, then turned to the boy, running his hands over the silver material approximating a windshield on his new stuffed bike.

``Bye, Aaron,'' she said, leaning over to kiss him again as he turned his chubby cheek from her slightly.

``Bye, Mommy.''

``I know, it was supposed to be our day,'' she started.

Nick touched her hand.

``We'll be fine. Tell her I said `hi,' and not to worry, everything is going to be alright.''

She nodded, then turned and walked away. Her tall, thin frame faded into a dark blob against the light streaming in through the glass doors. It gained definition again passing to the outside, as she reached into her purse and pulled out her cell phone before disappearing around the corner.

``Why does Mommy always have to go?'' Aaron asked, still looking down at the bike.

``Well, buddy, Aunt Julie has been unhappy lately and Mommy is helping her cheer up. You know That's important, right? Helping other people?''

``Yeah.''

``Someday you'll have a little brother or sister and when they're feeling sad you'll get to help them too.''

``Okay.''

He really couldn't understand, but what did Nick expect? While he was a pretty smart kid, he was just a little under three.

He sat there silent for a time, as Nick tried to distract him with games, to no avail. Nick glanced around looking for a way to change the subject. Fortunately, he found one powerful enough to gain the boy's attention.

``You know, all this talking is making me hungry again. I think I might need some ice cream.''

``Ice cream?''

``Yeah, ice cream. Do you want some ice cream?''

``Uh huh.''

``Okay, but you've got to promise me something.''

``Uh huh.'' His eyes were in high beam mode, panning over to the counter.

``Promise you'll be nice to Mommy when she gets back, okay?''

``Okay.''

``Mommy is being very helpful to Aunt Julie. I know you miss her. I do too. But what she's doing is very important. Okay?''

``Okay.''

Two incredibly sloppy sundaes and five minutes of clean-up later, they left to head across the street and explore the mall. They had roughly four hours to kill before meeting Marisol, and with the temperature blazing over 100, an air-conditioned enclosure filled with visual stimuli was as good a place as any to pass the time.

It had been a while since they'd really walked around a mall. Most of the time their visits were in and out, zipping into an anchor store to shop or a restaurant to get some food, beeline to one or two other spots and then leaving, on to the next thing on the Sunday ''honey do'' list.

During Nick's pre-teen and early teen years, this was his haunt, he thought. An exotic village with endless possibilities.

Video games.

Batting cages.

Photo booths.

Miniature golf.

Movies.

Then they'd head to the food court, where three large boxes of fries could fuel an hour of gawking at wandering gaggles of girls, followed by conversation and endless speculation on just what it would take to win the hearts of the blossoming Venuses who had been all but invisible to them just a few months before, and then, suddenly, seemed to be everywhere, and occupying a quickly growing amount of their attention and ardor.

Journeying around the mall with four hours to kill and a restless almost three-year-old on your hands was another matter entirely, one which required an intense concentration.

The bookstore, minus leering at the top shelf, was a must. Time tore by when it was spent playing with Paddington bears and reading Elmo books while sitting in beanbag chairs on a kaleidoscope rug.

Watching Aaron read, or at least attempt to, was one of the joys of Nick's life. Seeing him glance intently at the pages, his lips open and barely, sorta, moving along, his big sky blue eyes darting from space to space, eating up new information, was magical. At home, Nick would follow along, helping him shape the syllables, place the words. Being there as these formerly intimidating, alien symbols were tamed and transformed into keys to a once-secret universe was one of the man's favorite activities.

But in public it was quite different. Aaron exerted his independence, wanting Daddy nearby but not too close.

``Me do it meself,'' he would say.

And he would, in his own way. Recognizing a few of the familiar items in the pictures and making up the rest to his satisfaction. Putting the pieces together slowly but surely, while giving his imagination a workout. Learning to read.

And as Nick listened to his cobbled stories, more complex and fantastic than the simplistic fables committed to paper before him, a part of him wished that those could remain the boy's view of the tales. A part of Nick was sad about the boy losing those improvised wonderments once he gained knowledge, once he was conditioned to see what those sentences meant, their alignment defining reality rather than merely acting as a framework to what he wanted to see.

About an hour later, with a small plastic tote of three tomes in tow, Aaron took Nick's hand as they walked out into the mall, sharing a mushy, sickly sweet vanilla ice drink masquerading as something to do with coffee, minus actual coffee. The Lite Brite-colored mini-amusement park in the center of the mall was their next destination. With its softly bucking broncos, saddles at arms' height, miniature cars and a strange polar-bear-shaped bus, it was a haven for small children and their parents, always ready with more quarters to buy themselves some more time.

Like Nick, Aaron was always drawn to the polar bear bus off to the left side, near the chipped, blue Etch-A-Sketch photo booth. The bizarre, icy fiberglass beast had a layer of shiny, powder blue -and-ivory hair around the bear's chassis. Its body was solid and enveloping, with cracking, burgundy leather seats trimmed in a fingerprint-smudged gold, sitting within where the bear's body would be.

Thick paws at the fore and shank, it had serene, dark blue glass eyes and a sweet smile on its face that was comforting. But its incongruity -- a half-animal, half-machine in the midst of several more traditional vehicles (albeit machines with human characteristics like smiley grills and cartoon eye headlights) -- made it stand apart.

Nick put Aaron aboard it, strapped him in with the flimsy seat belt, dumped a handful of quarters into the slot and watched him smile as the bear's voice said ``all aboard!'' and it began to slowly lurch and chug.

``He looks just like you,'' a tan, dark-haired twentysomething woman, said, as Nick stood back from the ride.

``Thanks,'' Nick said. And he did. Tousled blonde hair, blue eyes, a little sun giving him some color, sturdy build.

He wasn't Nick's biological son. He had only started dating Marisol when the boy was nine months old. But he was Nick's son. At least he thought of him that way. And when he looked at Marisol, with her pale skin and burnt sienna hair, and thought of Aaron's ``real dad,'' Justin, all short, dark and swarthy, Nick wondered if there hadn't been some sort of weird physiological transference taking place in which the boy inherited some of Nick's genes through close proximity and emotional contact.

``You seem to really get along well.''

``He's a fun little guy to hang out with,'' Nick said, glancing back at Aaron waving to him.

``It's nice to have a Dad who takes time out to play with his kids,'' she added, with a long look at Nick and then a quick one back at her children on the taxicab ride.

``Yeah, I guess it is,'' Nick said, smiling and watching Aaron push on a red button in front of him to clink a bell in the bear's red hat.

"It is, trust me, it's nice to see," she said, smiling. She was standing nearer, thin and athletic, just a bit over five-foot-tall, in a stylish top and capri pants, as Nick stood back from the ride.

At that point, a girl who was obviously the tanned woman's daughter jumped off the ride and came running towards her. She was a tall child of about five or six, with immaculate brown hair, a kitten's-tongue-pink ribbon running through it, and a white cotton dress dancing with thin, frothy pink lines of bears.

``Mommy, can we go to the Skee-Ball now?'' she plead, and her mother nodded.

"Now, she looks very much like you!" Nick said.

"Thanks!" she smiled, and turned to her mini-me.

"You want to go to Skee-Ball? The one at Video Game Central?"

"Yeah? What other one is there?" she gave her Mom a quizzical look.

"Well, duty calls," the mother said, smiling and winking as she walked away. "Have fun!"

"I'm sure I will," Nick said, looking back at Aaron pumping his fist and belting out "Choo! Choo!"

Another child of around eight or nine, part of a pack of three, all chewing large ropes of licorice, jumped on the back of the polar bear ride and jumped off quickly.

"Pee-ewwww!" the kid said, waving his hand in front of his nose and looking at Nick. "I think your kid pooped his pants."

Aaron laughed.

Duty called.

The next stop was one Nick was sort of dreading, since it would be considerably more complicated. But it had to be done.

The bathroom.

A quick couple of pats on the behind revealed that, at least to this point, the stench was only a warning shot, a harbinger.

In common parliance, a fart.

But Nick knew it was only a matter of time before it was more, so they started in the direction of the restrooms.

It's always something of an odd juggling act bringing a small boy into a bathroom with you, wondering whether there was going to be a changing station, and if not, how tricky it would be to get the diaper switch done. And it was especially strained when said child usually insists on singing a song about his ``winky'' as he drops trou and training diaper.

Unfortunately, that would be the least of Nick's worries on this trip.

By the time they'd gotten into the long hallway leading to the men's restrooms it was obvious they were too late.

``Uh oh,'' Aaron said as a rocket sound boomed in his pants.

A growing stain formed in the seat of his jeans, one that defiantly spread out above and below the diaper lines and darkened the yellow tractor on his back pocket.

"Uh, oh," he echoed.

Nick couldn't have put it better himself.

Getting him onto the too-small diaper changing shelf in the bathroom, and being thankful that there was one in the men's room at all, Nick soon realized how dire the situation was. To put it discreetly, the diaper stood no chance against an onslaught Nick would later theorize to be dairy-fueled. Aaron's pants and shirt were the casualties of his digestive war and a large part of his lower back and legs were covered in a creeping goo that smelled worse than anything Nick had had the displeasure to experience in his life up to that point.

There was only one way out of this, and it was not going to be pretty.

In the side pockets of Nick's khaki cargo shorts, he was always prepared with no fewer than five spare diapers for a trip this long. But with Marisol's disappearance, it had turned out much longer than expected. He'd already gone through two diapers just during the trek to the "fun time place," the second of which had just fallen victim as they were quickly making our way to the bathroom.

The third was on Aaron for all of a minute as he stood next to Nick, while the man started soaking the boy's clothes in the sink.

"Boom!" the boy laughed, when the bomb dropped to take out diaper number three, his next salvos splattered forth in quick defiance of Nick's handiwork.

Down to two.

Whispering a silent prayer to whatever deity handles the blessings of this type, Nick put the fourth dipe on him, and hoped for the best. Aaron stood next to him, a small boy Winnie the Pooh-ing it, clad only in a shirt, diaper, socks and shoes, as Nick quickly scrubbed the boy's small pants with the pink hand soap, and people shuffled in and out of the bathroom giving them strange looks.

"Why is everyone looking at us, Daddy?"

"Because we're just that handsome, pal."

"Oh."

"Yup."

"Uh-oh."

He looked up at Nick. "I sorry."

And at that point, diaper four was done, and this time, the splatter took out the back bottom of his shirt as well.

Nick was down to his last bullet. He had to think fast.

Leaving Aaron's shirt and pants soaking in the sink, he tore off a long skein of paper towels and doused them in soap and water. Whipping the defiled diaper off him and chucking it in the trash can, Nick did a quick wipe of Aaron's back with the towels, threw them away and carried his now-buck-naked-except-for-the-shoes companion into the far stall.

Nick reached for the seat liners. Out. Reached for the toilet paper. Out.

``Stay here Aaron. Stay right here. Stand right here."

Aaron stood there naked and laughing as Nick lurched out the door and into the next stall, which was, thankfully, unoccupied.

Three rolls of paper, two of them stripped to the cardboard. The third, paydirt. Nick whirled it around, collecting as much as he could.

``Winky! Winky! Winky!'' Aaron danced around the stall, cupping his boyhood in his hand.

A scarecrow-thin teenager with red, moppish hair and braces walked in, gave them a strange look, took one whiff and made a beeline for the urinal, pulling his shirt up over his nose as an impromptu gas mask.

Brandishing a gigantic bouquet of unrolled toilet paper, Nick bounded back towards Aaron's stall. Too late. Seconds too late. It was like one of those slow motion sequences in a Bruce Willis movie where he dives to stop the bullets from hitting their target, a deep ``Noooooooooo'' tragically draining from his maw.

``Uh oh,'' Aaron said, as he inadvertently decorated the floor and wall of the stall like a Jackson Pollock painting.

Not taking any chances, Nick rushed to wipe off the toilet seat and put down a thin ring of paper. Grabbing him, Nick set the boy down on there. As he'd been instructed at home, as part of his ongoing training, Aaron grasped ahold of the side to avoid falling in. Just in time. He giggled as the next round fortunately hit its proper mark.

``Poop! Poop!'' he said, as Nick jetted out to grab more paper towels for the massive clean-up.

``Stay right there, Aaron.''

With at least one rainforest bunched in both hands, Nick closed the stall door behind him and got to work sopping up the mess. Seeing him pulling his t-shirt up over his nose in a useless attempt to block the ripe aroma made Aaron explode in laughter.

``Daddy, you look funny!''

``Stay there, Aaron. Hold on.''

``Daddy looks funny!''

Fortunately, throughout the toxic waste duty, Aaron remained hunched over, doing his business, which amused him to no end.

``Poop!''

``Poop!''

``Poop!''

With each shower into the basin he added his own unique color commentary.

``Thanks for the update, buddy,'' Nick said, scrubbing the last of the mess off the floor.

Nick didn't keep exact track, but at least a half-dozen other people came and left the bathroom during that time, as he piled up paper, making regular deposits into the tank under Aaron, flushing it down and going back for another round.

With only one diaper left and the closest store where he could replenish their supply being the big box down the road from the mall, Nick had no choice but to wait it out. Keep him there until the storm had abated. Finally, it seemed like it had.

"No more poop."

"Are you sure?"

He looked down.

"No more poop."

"Ok. Stay there, Aaron."

Nick opened the door and darted toward the sink, to wring out the clothing left there, grab some more towels and attempt to dry it out for the dangerous trek to the store.

But when he lunged to grab it ... it was gone.

A few minutes before, when he was otherwise occupied, he'd barely noticed a round of what sounded like pre-teen kids cackling in between intermittent whispers. With other things on his mind, obviously, he thought little of it.

He should have thought more.

After all, Nick thought, he was that age once. A wild, post-larval savage loose at the mall, bored and looking for trouble. And as much as he was pissed when he saw the empty sink, he knew deep down that when he was twelve or thirteen, with a face full of acne and a head full of devious schemes, or at least practical jokes, this was exactly something he and his friends would have done.

Karma. Damn it.

Momentarily defeated, Nick slunk back to the stall, where he waited Aaron out. About forty-five minutes later, when he seemed wrung, Nick washed him up, dried him and carefully put on the last diaper.

``Okay, buddy, we're going on a little ride,'' Nick said. ``Hold on tight.''

``Where did my clothes go, Daddy?''

``Some bad guys stole them, buddy. We're going to get you new ones.''

He seemed puzzled, but that was better than upset.

Saying another silent prayer, Nick grabbed Aaron in his arms and bolted down the hallway, through the mall. A messy-haired grown man looking like a ragamuffin in a drenched, sweaty t-shirt and shorts, carrying a baby with his hair wet and slicked back, wearing only a diaper. They looked like a bad sitcom duo from the White Trash Network. Nick walked as briskly as he could, his arms wrapped around Aaron to keep him safe and warm, the strong smell of generic liquid soap trailing behind them.

They made it past the bookstore.

They made it past the mini-golf.

They finally made it past the movie theater and to the door.

And then the smell.

Nick's hand instinctively reached down. Nothing.

``Aaron, did you?''

``No poop, Daddy, just toot.''

``Okay, good.''

Car in sight, Nick clenched his right arm around Aaron tighter as he reached his left hand into his pocket, grabbing the keychain and clicking the remote. The car was open.

Front seat up.

Into the car seat.

Belts fastened. He's in.

Front seat down.

The smell again.

``Aaron?''

``Toot!''

Nick ran around to the other side. Car door open. In. Start. Seat belt. Quick look back. Clear. Pulled out. Pulled away. Looking frantically to either side, zipping through the parking lot, past the intersection, onto the street, down the street, hit the light.

``Please, please, please . . .''

Green. Past the light.

Uh oh.

``Aaron?''

``Toot!''

Into the turn. To the next light. Green. There is a God.

Onto the straightaway, around the curve, into the home stretch. Parking lot. There's a spot. It's close. Got it. In.

Brake. Park. Stop. Keys. Door open. Closed. His door open. Front seat up. Belt off. Toddler out of his chair. Door closed and locked. Brisk walk through the parking lot. Through the automatic doors, into the store.

``Welcome to SuperMart,'' the lady extends her arm and Nick grabs the flyer, to be polite, and, also, just in case. He might need it.

``Aaron?''

``Uhhhh . . .''

This one had some force behind it. Nick felt something slimy on his forearm and shirt. He looked down. I'm hit, he thought. Something, but not much. He wiped off his arm on his shirt.

Nothing compared to the rest. Maybe Aaron's hit a lull. Maybe he's drained. Hopefully.

``Try to hold it Aaron. We're almost there.''

Make it to the kids department and grab the first shirt and shorts seen in his size. Haul a pack of diapers off the shelf and stuff them under Nick's arm. Grab a pack of baby wipes and do the same.

An older lady with fat, square glasses, teal eye-shadow slathered above raccoon eyes, salami-colored skin, boobs like melted wax and a paunch that looked like a bowling ball under her Lynyrd Skynyrd tank top gave Nick a look to maim. A dishwater blonde teen with an inch of dark brown roots, acid-wash jean shorts sliced up to her ass curve and not quite covering her ass crack, a hot pink tube top and fresh bruises down her pale right arm chomped her gum in Nick's direction.

``Mister you gotta git that there baby some clothes.''

``Thanks for the tip.''

Nick got a quick look at himself in a mirror whizzing by the dressing room. Red-faced, scarecrow hair, shirt doused in sweat and painted down the middle with slime, cradling a stained diaper baby in one arm and a pack of dipes, a pack of wipes, a pair of My First Budweiser shorts and a tiny t-shirt that says, ``My Daddy Gits Er Dunn!'' under his other.

``Daddy . . .''

``Just a few more seconds, Aaron. Hold on just a few more seconds.''

On the way to the register, just before, Nick passed by the men's department and saw a rack of black t-shirts. The first large he saw, he lifted to add to his burden, then put back down.

Nick shook his head, and uttered, "I don't care how desperate I am, I'm not buying a shirt that says, ``Free Mammograms! Sign Up Here'' with an arrow pointing downward."

Then he heard it.

Damn!

``Aaron?''

``Toot!''

He grabbed the next large t-shirt he saw. It had a girl's dark, smiling face silk-screened on it. She was winking under palm fronds over her head. Next to her is the slogan, ``Get Lei'ed in Hawaii!''

They zoomed into the express lane. A middle-aged woman in a striped shirt took one look at Nick and the child and stepped aside, putting her items back into her basket.

``You can go ahead of me,'' she said, her face pursed in disgust.

"Thanks!"

The cashier raised her eyebrows and scowled as Nick dumped his clothing and diapers on the counter and she whisked it with as little finger contact possible over the barcode-reader and into plastic bags.

``We're almost home free, buddy. Just hold on. Just hold on.''

Chomping her gum condescendingly, she clicked a red button with long, fake, bedazzled fingernails and spewed Nick a total. He whisked his card, signed, got his receipt, quickly stuffed it and his card in his pocket, grabbed the bags and breathed out heavily. Only fifty feet away from the washroom and salvation.

``Daddy?''

``Aaron . . .''

Oh no.

And now it becomes a sprint, the bags flailing around Nick's arms, the boy gritting his teeth and concentrating, trying to keep it all inside, and thankfully, at least doing so until they got into the bathroom, into a stall, and at the last possible second onto a toilet. Again. The door not closed yet, but yup, at least inside and down, until he turned into a little sprinkler.

Another half-hour of waiting later and they seemed to be fine. From the looks of things he'd gotten it all out. They'd gone a whole twenty minutes without an incident and even the warning shots had dissipated, a hopeful omen of things to come. Or, not to come.

Just to be sure, Nick left him on the toilet, at the ready just in case, hanging onto the toilet seat, singing a song he learned from a big green muppet, as Nick cleaned himself up, attempting to make himself look somewhat presentable in his brand new t-shirt.

Then it was on to cleaning up Aaron.

Nick didn't make the same mistake he had in the mall bathroom. Instead, he plucked Aaron up off the toilet and commandeered the sink area, with his old shirt soaking in one basin as he washed Aaron off, dabbing a chunk of paper towels into soapy water in the basin right next to it.

An employee walked in. He took one disinterested look at the shirtless man towel-bathing the naked child and attended to his own business, sauntering out whistling without washing his hands. Nick got the feeling he'd seen this before.

With Aaron finally clean, diapered up, dressed, and ready to go, and Nick in his new wardrobe, Nick picked him up in one arm, bags draped over the other, and beat a path to the door, avoiding any eye contact all the way to the car, where Nick strapped him into his booster without event. They were ten minutes early when they got to their reservation that evening at Jungle Bungle and walked inside.

No sign of Marisol.

Nick checked his cell phone.

No calls.

Twenty-five minutes later, Marisol arrived, still without having called to say why she was late. She breezed in on an invisible but unmistakable cloud of nicotine residue, bobbing her head and muttering vague exasperations about her sister. Aaron was playing in a netted cage full of multi-colored plastic balls with three other kids, but nonetheless, in the midst of his reverie, he noticed her immediately. He left the play area and toddled over to her for a hug.

``What's he wearing?'' she looked at Nick. ``Wait, what are you wearing?''

``It's a long story.''

``Did you and Daddy go shopping?''

``Yeah, we went to Super-Mart.''

``That sounds fun.''

``Uh huh.''

She glanced at Nick. ``So, did you make the payment, for the trip?''

``Oh, man,'' Nick slumped down into his chair. ``With everything that happened, I totally forgot!''

``Geez, Nick, what . . .''

``Don't worry, I'll do it tomorrow.''

``Are they still open tomorrow?''

``Yeah, they should be. I'll take it then.''

``Fine, I guess,'' she exhaled pointedly and sat down, pouring herself a glass of soda from the pitcher.

``So, other than that,'' she sighed, "everything was fine?''

Nick looked down at Aaron, happily sipping 7-Up from a purple-and-white striped straw, his chubby little arms drowning in an oversized t-shirt, emblazoned with one phrase in big red letters.

``My Daddy Gits Er Dunn!''

``Yeah,'' Nick said. ``It's all good.''

NINE

It's not such a bad day to die, Simon thought.

The backdrop for an exit was gorgeous. The skies were exploding with oranges and pinks and purples over bleeding blues and the patchwork of earth beneath them – the one the plane was currently hurtling towards – was an elegant quilt of crimson and gold and green grids waiting to catch the screeching cross of metal they were snugly wrapped in.

It was a good time, too. Just short of thirty. Single. No kids. Lots of money to leave to his family to pay for a funeral. And right at the tail end of a trip to Las Vegas, coming home after a week of fun and a job interview. Down to the final two. Fifty percent chance. He could die thinking he was going to get the job and slip into the netherworld on a fantasy of how amazing his life would've been.

He was enjoying the view when a bright flash of sun filled the cabin, enough to make him and the other passengers cover their eyes. Before they knew it, there were strange sounds, the buzz of the crew scurrying, a few firm and reassuring announcements, the low hum of uncomfortable conversations and a wave of deep breaths as everyone strapped themselves in and braced for the worst while hoping for the best.

``Don't worry about it," the relaxed older guy next to Simon said, apparently responding to Simon's absent-minded nail-biting as he looked out the window, seeking a clue, a sign, as to what was going to happen next.

``Why not?" Simon asked, hoping for a good answer.

``I've been through this before, plenty of times, and I've been fine, so does that answer your question?" he smiled, raising an eyebrow.

``No, not really," Simon nervously said.

The older man looked at Simon, paused for a moment.

"Okay."

"Okay, what?"

``Listen," the older man began, "I've been in planes shot down over enemy territory, I've been in puddle jumpers that lost an engine, I've been in big boys like this that'll rock and fall. There are a lotta ways you can go down, but, there are a lot of times, more times, you're not. Because things like this happen all the time, and the guys in charge have seen things like this happen all the time, and even if they haven't experienced it themselves, they've heard about it, and they're here to deal with it."

``Yeah, but..."

He stopped the younger man.

``Hey," he said. ``You think they want to die any more than you do?"

Hmm. He couldn't say. For some reason Simon imagined a pilot coming home to his wife astride his best friend, telling him that she's sold all his stuff and the kids have moved to Zimbabue, leaving him just enough money in his pocket to grab a bottle on the way to work on this very flight.

``I guess not," Simon said.

``You guess not," he kind of chuckled in that low crackle of a guy who's smoked and drank a bit over his years. ``Listen, I was in a puddle jumper once, fuel tank goes out. Goes out. And I'm about your age, and I think, man, we're done for."

``So what happened?"

``Pilot doesn't blink an eye, doesn't get all worried or anything like that. He just says `no big deal, we just have to switch fuel tanks,' and we switch into glide while he does that and before long we're fine and we're flying. We get back and we're all okay and the pilot says goodbye to us like nothing ever happened. Says that's perfectly normal. That's why they carry two fuel tanks.''

``Yeah, but what about in between, when they're just gliding,'' Simon asked.

``Well, that's when you hope you have a good pilot,'' he said.

``Yeah,'' Simon said, ``well, hopefully, we've got one here.''

``Yeah,'' he said, paused, and added, ``only one way to tell.''

``How's that?''

``Well,'' he opened up his magazine, ``we'll know if the plane lands safely.''

"That's reassuring."

"It should be."

"What do you mean?"

"What I mean," the older man said, "is that it's something you have absolutely no control over, and because of that, you shouldn't sweat it. After all, what's the point? You can't control it, you're not going to suddenly get control over it, so why bother wasting time worrying about it?"

"I guess that makes sense."

"Listen, there are enough things in your life that you can control, that you should concern yourself with," the man said. "Don't complicate things by adding a whole bunch of stuff that you can't do anything about."

"Fair enough," Simon said, somewhat distantly. He knew little to nothing about planes, other than how to board and fly on them. For all he knew, this guy was completely full of crap. He could've told him that a magical Leprechaun lived above the cockpit, and as long as the pilot carried a baggie of Lucky Charms, they would be golden.

But the more he thought about it, beyond any technicalities, the guy had a point.

Simon scanned his life over the last year, thought about all the times he'd stressed out about something that ultimately ended up being resolved in a positive or neutral fashion. But even if it didn't, his worrying wouldn't have changed the outcome either way.

"So, what brought you to Vegas?" the older man asked.

"Job interview. And just, Vegas."

"Just Vegas brings a lot of people in," the man laughed.

"You live there?" Simon asked.

"Among other places," the man said.

"Do a lot of traveling?"

"Yeah. All part of the job," the man said. "So, is it a good job you're looking at?"

"Yeah, sure looks like it," Simon said. "I think so."

"Think you'll get it?"

"Sure. I think I did pretty well."

"Hope you'll get it?"

"Yeah," Simon said. "Vegas would be a cool place to live. But, I don't have to tell you that."

"Where do you live now?"

"Chicago. I'm flying home."

"Chicago's not so bad either," the older man said.

"No, it isn't," Simon said. "I can live without the weather though. I just moved back there a year ago, after bouncing around Southern California for a while. I grew up around Chicago, but man, California was nice."

"Yeah, but the change of seasons is good to have sometimes," the older man said. "Keeps things interesting. Reminds you of your place in time."

"Yeah, I guess," Simon said. "I mean, at this point, it's weird to imagine having Christmas without snow or fall without all the leaves again."

"Yeah, that first snowfall is pretty amazing, and it's nice, especially around Christmastime," the older man said.

For some reason Simon couldn't explain, a memory of his childhood flashed into his head, fully formed, as if coming from a movie camera. A picture of him waking up with his brother and sister, looking out the window and seeing the sea of glimmering white across his yard, shimmering in the morning sunlight, as he filled with excitement thinking of all of the wonderful games they were going to play that day, all because that pristine, magical blanket had dropped, heavy and hardy, upon the torn, gray, frazzled up, ripped bare ground they'd left behind when they went to sleep.

"But then, of course, it's followed by all the dirt and sludge and black ice and horrid weather for the next three or four months," Simon added, throttling his armrest with a feverish grip as the plane sloshed and jutted about. "Holy crap! Do you think the pilot's got a death wish or something?"

The older man laughed. "Not many people do. I wouldn't worry about it."

"I don't know," Simon said. "I think it's more than you'd like to admit."

"Really?"

"You'd be surprised."

"Doubtful."

Simon looked at the man and shook his head.

"Let me ask you a question," the man said, taking a big gulp of his drink.

"Do I really have a choice?" Simon replied.

The older man laughed. "Not really, you're pretty much stuck with me until the end of the flight."

"Okay, then ask," Simon said.

The older man leaned forward a bit, arched his eyebrow.

"Have you ever wanted to die?"

Simon stiffened a bit in his seat and unconsciously edged away from the older man.

"No."

"Never? You've never been so depressed, so down, so dejected, that you've wanted to kill yourself, or just wished you were dead?"

"No."

Simon looked away. The older man looked over, raised his eyebrow and took a drink, knocking it down as the ice cubes jangled against each other, then motioned to the stewardess with a wink.

"Okay, maybe," Simon admitted.

"Yeah."

"But it's not what you'd think."

"Uh huh."

"I mean, it's not like it was after a breakup, or after some terrible personal tragedy or anything like that."

"Okay."

"Okay," Simon began to explain, "I was working in theater at the time. Production work. It's a noisy, sultry Sunday afternoon and we're inside the dark confines of The Verona Theater, as the life-and-death drama of 'Tuesdays With Morrie' is unfolding on stage. The real-life characters of Mitch Albom and Morrie Schwartz are exchanging last precious wisdoms as Morrie heads down the trail on the final weeks of his life, a victim of Lou Gerhig's disease.

"For the most part there isn't a dry eye in the house. The action on stage is heartbreaking.

"So, during intermission, it's just a wave of Kleenex, a snowstorm heading outside into a humidor. Sweltering August day. I step outside the darkened theater into the blinding daylight, and into a different kind of tragedy.

"Right across the street, hundreds of feet above the theater, on the steel broadcast tower of a TV station, another life-and-death drama is unfolding.

"A man is several stories up on the tower, threatening to jump.

"About four dozen people are gathered on the streets of downtown to watch as this man, in a green t-shirt, jeans, a baseball cap and sunglasses, considers whether or not to end his life.

"And not in a peaceful manner. In a painful, public, literally bone-crushing way.

"This is obviously not a decision entered into lightly.

"This is something that is the culmination of a significant trail of pain.

"And it all began while we were inside, oblivious, reliving another man's trail of pain. One that ended in a best-selling book, worldwide fame and a hit movie, rather than a forgotten story in a newspaper and several hours of mess needing to be cleaned up to erase a nasty stain.

"Over a half-dozen police cars and two fire trucks are parked along the side of the street, yet they couldn't do much but watch as the man contemplated a leap down through the jagged, crosshatched steel edifice to the concrete below.

"The actors and crew joined us outside, and the show ended up being put on hold as we gathered that this has been going on for close to an hour, so, as one bystander says, we ``got there for the good part."

"And it was, for the man, if not the spectators.

"Slowly, after some time alone high in the breeze, the sunlight, the man climbed down the tower and onto the roof of the channel 4 building, and then inside, and we never saw him again."

"Okay," the older man said, sipping his latest drink. "Happy ending. The guy climbed down. Why so morose about that?"

"Well," Simon said. "For one thing, it was a bizarre scene to watch unfold. Particularly since just a short time before I was watching a play that deals so poignantly with death. And the strange thing is, there was more emotional resonance on the inside of the theater.

"The man on the tower, and the entire scenario, didn't seem real. It took a while to really register that this was a human being, a person who was obviously disturbed, who was compelled by some inner demons so powerful and impacting that he felt driven to potentially take his own life.

"Yet with the police cars and witnesses standing by, it seemed more like a scene from a crime show.

"Now, in the meantime, inside the theater, you have two actors intimately re-enacting the lives of a pair of real-life people, and doing so with such tenderness and sensitivity that the room was awash in tears.

"The expression on most faces outside the theater?

"Wonder.

"Curiosity.

"Anticipation.

"Even a few smirks.

"And, most twisted of all, disappointment.

"Disappointment from some, many, that they'd spent that much time watching this unfold, and they weren't rewarded with death. Rather, they were 'let down,' as one of them put it.

"No tears.

"No relief.

"Disappointment.

"That a man with family, who was once born of a mother and father that may have loved him, a man who, at some point in his life, probably inspired a woman unrelated to him to care for him, to love him, who had friends, at some point, people who were connected enough to him to have some sort of emotional tie, to have an impact in his life, and for him to have an impact on theirs, was going to continue to have a chance, a chance to live, to breathe, to love, to have an impact on humanity.

"That same humanity watching him. Waiting. Wondering. Smirking. Disappointed.

"And watching all the people milling around, sullen like that, I couldn't help but think that maybe the guy had the right idea. I mean, why bother with this place and these people? Why not just pack it in and get out of this place and hope for something better on the other side."

The old man nodded his head a couple of times, took another drink and looked at Simon.

"Let me ask you another question," he said.

"Yeah?" replied Simon.

"Were all the people disappointed?"

"Huh?"

"Were all of them disappointed? Did all of them seem sullen and sad he didn't jump, or was it just a few?"

Simon thought about it for a moment.

"Actually, come to think of it, there were only a few people."

"And were there more people who breathed a sigh of relief, and seemed to be happy the guy didn't jump?"

"Well, actually, now that I think about it, yeah."

"But the ones who made the most profound impact on you, the ones who actually got you contemplating ending your own life, as you say, were the people who were disappointed."

Simon sighed and put his hand to his head, rubbing his temple and slinking back into his chair.

"Yeah."

The older man just smiled and shook his head.

"Kid, don't sweat it," he said. "You know what? Don't let the jerks control your life. There are always going to be jerks. Always. But don't let 'em have a vote on your happiness. Never let them turn your life into a democracy. Never let anyone turn your life into a democracy. Because there are always going to be people who are miserable, and there's nothing they like more than making sure that everyone else is right there with 'em, because it's the lazy way out and it's a lot easier dragging everyone else down to their level than them making the effort to raise themselves up to be happy."

"Yeah, well, whenever faced with a choice, humanity is apt to opt for the laziest way out," Simon said.

"Not always, and not all humanity," the older man said. "And ya know, the thing is, not even they want it that way. The cynics and the jerks and the critics are just a bunch of phonies, whistling in the dark, trying to hide their fear. Trying to pretend that they don't care, not because they don't, but because they're afraid of what might happen if they do, and because they don't have enough confidence in themselves to make that step. So, instead, they hide behind the usual phony poseur crap.

"Kid, life isn't about finding yourself, it's about creating yourself. It's about becoming the person you need to be. When it comes down to it, we're all really looking for the same things: to belong, to feel needed, to feel wanted, to feel a logic and basis for our lives, which are buffeted by uncertainty and illogic. We need destiny. We need place. That can be in parenting and guiding your child, it can be in doing your job or being part of an important relationship. But if we don't have it, and worse, if we try to fill it in substandard fashion, that's when we feel hollow and dissonant, and if we can't fill that space, we start to envy those that can. That's why it's so important to have the courage to strive for that, to find it, and to live it, regardless of what other people think.

"Everyone wants to believe the best, but most of the time, if you pass by twenty people on a street, we ignore the nine people who compliment us and the other ten people who don't say a word and obsess on the one idiot who insults us or says something to bring us down. Why is that person's opinion so important to us? Why should it count more than any of the others? Why are we so eager to believe the worst about ourselves when we should want to always believe the best? Shouldn't we instead live our lives believing the best for ourselves and discounting the worst, because in the end, that's what's going to make us happier and make our lives better?"

The man looked at Simon. There was a pause.

"I thought that was a hypothetical question," Simon said.

"Well," the older man said, with a tilt of his head as he finished his drink, "I guess whether it is, or it isn't, is up to you, isn't it?"

The man looked at his watch.

"Ya know, Simon, it doesn't matter if people don't believe in you. In the end all that matters is that you believe in yourself. It doesn't matter if people think you're right. What matters is that you can look at yourself in the mirror and know that what you're doing is for the right reasons."

Then, the plane rattled and rocked one last time, and smoothed out, once more gliding through the sun splattered skies.

Simon exhaled a huge sigh.

"Now where did all that worrying get you?" the man said.

"Pretty much the same place it got you," Simon replied, "just sitting here in the plane, only with bigger pit stains on my shirt."

"Exactly," the man grinned.

A light blipped on.

"I'll tell ya where those couple'a drinks got me," the man grumbled as he unbuckled his seat belt and stood up. "So if you'll be so kind as to excuse me..."

"Sure."

Simon stood up and let the man pass. While he was gone, Simon looked out the window at the wispy whiteness of the clouds, lolling by as he floated in space, just steps away, secure in a miracle of modern technology borne on a distant dream shoved into the world by a couple of stubborn bastards who didn't give a damn what anyone else thought.

The pilot announced they were arriving at their destination and with the polite beeps accompanying their way home, the older man returned to his seat, where he and Simon watched as they arced around and down onto the landing strip.

Shuffling laughs and small talk between them, Simon and the man disembarked and, along with the other chatting passengers, buzzed into the terminal, making their way to the baggage check.

"Don't you have anything to claim?" Simon asked, as the man began to walk away.

The man smiled and winked.

"I travel light."

He reached out to shake Simon's hand, held it tightly, and patted Simon on the shoulder and chest in a familiar, familial way. He looked at the younger man for a moment, settling on his face, his eyes, and smiled.

"Thanks for the time, kid."

Simon, under normal circumstances, might have felt odd, might have felt creeped out, might have been anxiously awaiting the man's exit, waiting until he got out of earshot so he could call Archer or Mistri or Faith or one of his other friends and tell them about the latest weirdo he'd met.

But he didn't.

He didn't feel any of the usual things he felt.

He felt, grateful.

"No, thank you," Simon said. "Really, it's been quite a trip. I appreciate it. Thanks for the advice."

"It's yours now, kid."

The man withdrew his hand.

"Have a good trip, Simon," he said. "Enjoy the ride."

"You too," the younger man nodded as the older man walked away.

Simon looked down at the baggage sliding by on the conveyor belt, then up at the man fading into the crowd.

"Hey!" Simon called. "I just realized – I never got your name!"

The man called back, a single word, with a slight wave and a smile, and was gone as a curtain of humanity closed about him.

"Stopwatch?" Simon scrunched his face. "Your name is Stopwatch?"

Simon watched the wheels on the belt turn around and around.

"Stop...watch... Stop..."

The luggage slumped out onto the conveyor belt, drifting by like hopeful suitors at a dance, waiting to be pulled away and claimed. Simon imagined them as teenagers from black and white sock hop photos, gleeful as their companions walked off with them, friends reunited with excitement, waiting to rejoin them on their journey.

"Wait, Stopwatch? Or... Pocket watch?"

Simon paced.

"Pocket watch?"

Hmm.

"Pocket watch."

Simon stopped.

"Seriously?" he thought. "You gotta be kidding me."

He patted his sport coat until he felt the tap of a circular object in his right jacket pocket, reached his hand in and pulled out an antique gold pocket watch he'd gotten from his late grandfather. And there, in the same pocket, was a business card.

Holding the watch in his right hand, he transferred the card to his left.

"Nice," Simon thought. "

He flipped the card over, expecting it to be glittery and gauche, emblazoned with a name like The Amazing Silverino or Henri Jacques Gilbertini, Magician of the Stars, plugging some off-strip burlesque and magic show where he performed slight-of-hand tricks, discreetly dipping business cards with his phone number written on them into the bejeweled brassieres of the cocktail waitresses.

 But it didn't.

It was pure white. One of the brightest whites he'd ever seen. And in a very faint, light grey type, just slightly raised, in a discreet, classic type, floated only one line.

Mr. Coddlesworth.

It took Simon a second to remember the name, and all that came with it, as his eyes glazed over and his mind popped at the coincidence -- it was a coincidence, right? -- and a smile grew on his face and he shook his head slightly in disbelief. He remembered himself as a child, and a ratty stuffed bear he took everywhere, and told everything, who had caught smiles and tears, who had held the warmth of his hugs and comforted him during dark nights, who had listened to his stories and his deepest fears, who was his best friend, and who had disappeared and caused him his first major heartbreak as a child.

And he reached down and slipped the card into his left jacket pocket and he tossed his gold pocket watch lightly in the air and caught it and flipped it open and looked at its face and smiled and looked up again.

Just in time.

To see his baggage having gone around the belt, drifting away, out of his reach, a sad, lonely hopeful without a match, slipping into the back again, waiting to come back around.

"Ahhhh. . . "

But Simon didn't finish his thought.

He didn't finish his sentence.

He didn't finish his gripe.

Because it was nothing he could control.

Unlike . . .

"Nice watch!"

"Huh?"

"Your pocket watch. I love it!"

Simon turned his head and the world went white.

White as the snow that childhood day, the wave waiting to be surfed.

White as the clouds seemingly holding his plane aloft.

White as the card with the name that made him pause.

Stop.

Watch.

And he saw her.

And she smiled.

And he smiled.

And he'd never seen her before, but instantly, he knew, he just knew, that he wanted to, at least, at least, for the foreseeable future.

And maybe, just maybe, for the non-foreseeable one as well.

TEN

William swallowed the last pill, looked out the kitchen window at the birds devouring the new heap of seeds in the feeder, grinned and glanced at his watch.

11:08.

He would wait three more minutes to call.

He could feel her smiling at him. ``Don't be late,'' he could hear her saying. ``You're always late.''

He wouldn't be. Not this time. Superstitious or not, it was maybe the last chance he had.

``It's 11:11," she said on their first date, so many years, decades, ago, yet it seemed to pass so quickly, still seemed not so long ago. ``Make a wish."

``Huh?"

``It's 11:11," she said, rubbing a finger over the face of her watch and silently contemplating her innermost desire for a few seconds. ``If you make a wish at 11:11 it has the best chance of coming true."

He wasn't sure if she was kidding or not. It didn't matter. It was an eccentric detail, part of the infectious joy she exuded, the magic she brought to his life. The ebullience that stood in such stark contrast to his driving, Spartan upbringing, that made him love her all the more. He shook his head and laughed it off, but that day, for the first time, he made a wish. That she would say yes if he asked her to go out with him again.

That night he was one for one. Batting 1.000.

From then on that ritual was part of their tapestry, the shared strangeness understood between a couple that ultimately binds all relationships.

Over the years many more wishes were made and his average dipped a bit under 1.000. No time more than in the past few years. But the early scrapbook days of their lives together were abundant in blessings, seeming requests granted. So he still felt he came out ahead for such little effort, sending a postcard out to the universe and waiting for a response.

The spring air carried the mingled scents of flowerbeds and lilac bushes heaving to life in through the sheer white curtains of the kitchen. The room flooded with the midday sun against the light yellow tiles and golden oak cabinets. It made for a comforting womb if the news was as he suspected it would be. But he couldn't stay here. Not in here. Not where she had collapsed.

Looking down at his watch again, nervously, he filled a large glass with water. He considered the message on the machine and was tempted to listen to it yet again, dissecting the intonation of the nurse's voice for any trace of emotion in her request.

``Hello Mr. Barstow, this is Jeanine from Dr. Calder's office. We have your test results and the doctor would like to speak with you regarding them. If you could give us a call at...''

Give them a call. Is that good? That they just want to talk to him on the phone? Certainly, they wouldn't give bad news over the phone, would they?

Or maybe they just want him to call so he can set up an appointment to talk to the doctor in person? Maybe that's what they would do? That wouldn't be good. In person is no good. It's never any good. It wasn't with Emily. It wouldn't be with him.

Besides, how could he wait? If they had bad news, he would rather just hear it over the line, know right away, rather than having to make the trip to go in and have them talk to him in person, have to dread every moment, have every possible negative scenario, the worst imaginable, run over and over in his head as he was getting ready and driving over. And what if they couldn't see him right away? Would he have to wait days for the result? They couldn't do that. They couldn't make him wait too long. Certainly, if it was something really bad, something life threatening, something that was going to kill him, slowly or quickly, they would have to tell him right away. Especially if it was something that was going to kill him quickly, because it wouldn't be fair if they waited because in waiting he would have even less time to prepare, even less time of awareness, to know that he was living in the last moments of his life.

Maybe even less time than Emily.

He tried not to think about it. He tried not to think about her for a second. Tried.

Cradling the cordless phone in one hand and the full container of water in the other he strolled towards the sun room to water the jungle of plants spiking up and draping over their pots amidst the bookshelves jammed with thick, colorful tomes.

His eyes teared a bit as he entered the room. The space still carried the musk of his last dog, Gretzky, and stray furs lingered in the creases and crunched folds of its furniture. Mornings, the two of them would relax. William with the papers, his customary science-fiction or spy novel, a pot of tea and a breakfast heavy with fresh herbs and vegetables plucked from the garden on the patio; his thick, jowly Mastiff with a generous bowl of kibble, rice and chicken and a slobbery toy or rawhide bone for dessert.

The tender beast was good company, particularly after Emily had gone, but he was a notorious shedder. No matter how much they had tried to brush him, no matter how often, it didn't seem to matter. And finally, towards the end, when the hard bristles' caresses against his throbbing joints would cause him to droop and whine, no matter how gingerly William attempted to groom him, they surrendered to the mess. Better to have his steadfast companionship in a halo of molting fluff than to sacrifice his comfort for their vanity.

In the weeks after Emily had died, Gretzky was a constant presence at his friend's side. He followed William everywhere around the house, lumbering just behind him, seeming to hang on his every word. William talked to him constantly, telling the dog about how much he missed his wife, detailing every little thing he longed for about her.

The way her laugh crinkled her crow's feet and she would have to dab a tear away if she was laughing really hard. The way she stood, with her hands on her hips, with that determined little girl look when she looked out on the yard every day and considered what she might do in her garden. The way she couldn't help touching him whenever they were near, putting her hand in his or her arm around him, or even playfully tapping him when he said something silly.

Sometimes William's words would sag into soft sobs. He would sit down and the dog would nudge his massive, fuzzy face against his leg. William would begin to pet him and eventually, his heartbeat would become calm, in metronome with the dog's slow, contented breathing.

The two weeks after Emily's funeral, after their other children had flown back across the country to their homes, their oldest son, Nick, had taken up residence in the extra bedroom. Just to be there, so they could distract each other with baseball statistics and lines from old movies. They went to the games and the race track, took trips to the Chinese restaurant to have food Emily couldn't eat because of her allergy. Always moving, keeping a blur, divorcing themselves from things that would remind them of her. It was a valiant effort, albeit with predictable results.

And there on the floor beside William, every night, in the bed he couldn't avoid, spread out in a large wicker dog bed filled with inviting comforters and sheets, was Gretzky. He would sit upright for William to pet his head as he fell asleep, and then collapse in a happy heap when the man withdrew his arm just before floating into slumber.

It was there, eleven months later, that William first heard Gretzky whine, noticed he was having a hard time standing up on his own. The vet had said this might happen, just as he said that upping the dosage of his pills could end up causing even further damage inside.

It wasn't long after that.

When the time finally came, when he could no longer bear to see his friend being inexorably eclipsed by pain, William called the vet, made the appointment and sadly counted down fourteen days. Those last two weeks were devoted to cultivating and bathing in Gretzky's buoyant, slobbery aura. Long rides with the windows down. Trips to the park. His own dishes of ice cream. An endless supply of fresh rawhides and toys with squeakers that made his ears perk and his eyebrows spread. And while watching TV or reading a book, hours of William running his hands over the velvety fur on the top of Gretzky's head, the dog's favorite spot, stopping to scratch behind the ears as the Mastiff's eyes slunk half-shut and he panted happily.

In truth it hadn't been measurably different than their lives together since Emily had gone. But it was pursued with a thirst for detail to commit to memory, to allow him to linger on in the ether of William's mind with a more palpable presence beyond his time.

When his day came, William couldn't hold back the tears. When they got to the hospital, he struggled with the decision until he looked again at the X-ray, saw the mass taking his companion over, realized that he couldn't force his boy to endure any longer for his sake.

With William by his side, lovingly rubbing his belly, his favorite spot, the needle went in and Gretzky, for the first time in such a circumstance, didn't flinch.

``Good boy,'' the nurse said, patting his head.

``Yes, he is,'' William said. ``Yes, he is. That's my boy. That's my Gretzky.''

And then, the dog's smile closed, his wet eyes shuttered, and he was gone.

Nick had been waiting for William in the lobby, to take him home. Surprising his father, he had taken his vacation during this time, to spend it with William, the way he had taken leave the year before, when his mother had died. As Nick had correctly figured, the loss had ripped open the still unhealed wound of his mother's death, and his father needed him by his side, at least until he had gotten over the initial wound.

They had talked of getting another dog, a puppy, or perhaps rescuing a stray from the pound, but in the end it was only Nick that ended up going home with three new pets, saving each from the same fate as Gretzky, albeit perhaps before their time.

William chose to remain alone, for the while. Better not to be attached to anything than to lose it, he said. Especially if he were to lose it quickly. That, he couldn't take.

With Emily, as with Gretzky, there hadn't been much time before the end. A trip to the E.R. A battery of tests. No call, no wait, a result after a day in the hospital.

Three months left, they said.

Three months.

The doctor was amazed she hadn't come in sooner, hadn't complained more about the pain. He marveled that she had been able to keep going.

It wouldn't have mattered when they had caught it anyway, he said. She was being devoured and it couldn't have been stopped.

It wasn't fair, William insisted. It wasn't fair. Wasn't fair that so many years would have to be reduced to three months. Especially when they had only just retired a few years before, when they had had so many plans, so many adventures, so many things to do, things they had worked for, saved for, strived for, places to go, a world to share.

And then, a cough.

Nothing, she said.

Nothing.

Then she folded to the floor one day with a thud, coughing uncontrollably, splattering the yellow floor of the kitchen with little dark red flecks, with the dog woofing deeply as William sped through 9-1-1, ``come on come on come on'' and the answer and the cry, quickly, quickly, send an ambulance, okay and he dropped the phone and the dog quit woofing and stood sentinel as he dropped to a knee over her and held her hand and told her he loved her and told her to hold on, hold on, hold on until they got here and he could get her to a hospital, and then the bell and the dog woofing and sorry Gretzky and the sunroom door closed with the dog behind it so the strangers could come in with their tubes and their bags and their boxes of things to attach to her as they pulled her up on the big silver tray, pulled her up and out into the back of the truck as William slammed the door shut behind as they strapped her in, and William pulled up into the back with her and them slamming the door shut behind him and speeding off in the direction of the hospital finally getting there and yanking her in and the calls from the people at the desk and in the line with them and getting her into the room and hooking her up and she's fine she's not having an attack but we're going to have to do tests and ``I love you'' and ``I love you too'' and ``I'll see you later honey'' and ``Please don't go'' he said to her feeling bad about being such a fatalist but saying what he couldn't help but feel as it came to his mind, flooding out of him exploding from his heart and her reassuring squeeze of his hand and ``Don't worry I'm not going anywhere'' and a wink and he felt better and she was ready and gone on a chair as they told him to wait a while.

And wait.

And wait.

Phone calls were made, arrangements, requests left with family members. Come by, yes. Could you please do us a favor and stop by to let the dog out and feed him, thanks. And yes, she's going to be fine they said, she's going to be fine.

She's going to be fine.

And then, she's not.

One trip canceled, another one scheduled. And then another. And then a third to another place, when he knew the answer, knew it deep down, but couldn't bear it, couldn't tolerate it, couldn't, until she said it was okay. She said it was time. She said it was going to be the same answer wherever they went, whatever path they took. Three trips taken, none of them expected, none of them lolled over on Sunday afternoons, none of them greeted by a rush of breath and a flush of dreams, planned out in candlelight, their bodies soft against one another on a Saturday night, her snug in his arms, her head on his chest, his fingers stroking her hair, his heart beating distant in her ear.

Three trips, each more manic than the one before.

And the one long discussed, to a foreign land of origin she'd never seen, the one never taken, would never be considered again.

Their remaining journey would be just as memorable, he promised.

Their last night at home, he cooked her favorite dinner for her, chicken cacciatore with extra garlic, as she put the finishing touches on another scrapbook, one detailing all the vacations they had taken together. After a meandering meal and sweet bowls of chocolate gelato and strawberries, they made love and they stayed awake in bed together late into the night, talking. About the first time they met. About their marriage, their children. About a lifetime of laughter echoing back to bring fond smiles and welcome tears.

At the onset of morning she woke suddenly, struggling. She couldn't breathe. A manic call. Another rush. Another trip to the hospital. This time the final one.

He hadn't even gotten the full three months with her.

Their waning moments together were spent in a large hospital bed. Her propped up, lying on her back, looking towards him. Him, scrunched on his side, next to her.

``What will I do without you?'' he said to her, holding her hand.

``I'll be with you,'' she said, voice fading. ``I'll be there... waiting for you, as always.''

She laughed weakly but stopped short, going motionless. Silent.

``I love you,'' he said. ``I love you.''

She didn't respond, but he wanted to think that she heard him, that it was the last thing she heard from him.

Then her chest dropped and she became smaller. And the room was filled with the rude whine of the machine and the distant sound of the clattering of hard shoes moving fast against the floor, louder and louder, to the door of her room.

The woman who was his entire life had been taken from him by a growing black hole on an X-ray.

One which had now, perhaps, finally spread its inky grasp out to him.

11:10.

Only one person knew. There was only one he could call and swear to secrecy knowing he would remain silent, optimistic, understanding. Nick. He loved his other children just the same but they had a far more difficult time dealing with tragedy. He loved them too much to string them along, waiting with him, for the results. But he had to tell someone, had to have a confidante, a rock, the only one remaining, and so he turned to Nick.

``They're just tests,'' the son said. ``Things could look exactly the same. It might not have metastasized; you might be exactly the same as you are. So don't get too worried about the whole thing.''

``I don't know,'' William replied. ``I think I might be joining your Mother soon. I just have a feeling, like she's been waiting.''

``Well, she always did say you were late for everything.''

He laughed.

``Don't worry, everything is going to be fine,'' Nick said before he got off the phone. ``Either way, everything is going to be fine.''

William looked at the clock to see it change. A good omen, he thought.

11:11.

He made his wish.

Then he dialed the hospital.

The nurse answered immediately, pleasantly, and asked him to hold on the line. Just a few seconds, and then the doctor took over, voice stern and matter-of-fact, demeanor hardly encouraging.

The numbers were high, he said, knowing William understood what that would mean.

He gave William more numbers. Elements of time. Quantities of dosage. Qualities of each increment he could seek to stretch and strain against the inevitable. Then, finally, another set of numbers. A day. A time. A room. More tests. Some hope. Some, but as William could tell by the words unsaid and the timbre of the doctor's voice, not much.

The conversation ended on an artificially up note, when both knew they were lying. But they were too polite to say anything about it.

The doctor hung up and the line went dead. William sat there with the phone in his hand until the silence emanating from it turned to brief static, then a captured voice repeated over and over and then to an insistent beep. Another rude push of sound, reminding him of an earlier day.

William stood up, breathed deeply, dropping his arms to his sides and letting the phone fall onto the couch. Far away from the receiver in the other room. He had three more phone calls to make, to his kids, and he knew they would not be easy.

He breathed heavily again, and looked around the room, remembering for a second when and where they had acquired each item. Some memories fast, some slow. For a moment his legs buckled, and he had to sit down, falling onto a chair and feeling the warmth of the soft saltwater down his cheeks.

Gaining himself again, he looked at the clock on the wall.

11:11.

Still.

It had stopped.

The battery had run out.

He laughed until he cried again, breaking down into sobbing, before collecting himself, his eyes red and raw, thinking about what he would say to the kids.

``Everything is going to be fine,'' Nick had said.

He reached for the phone. It had slid beneath a cushion. When he pulled it out, it was furry with leftover Gretzky hair stuck to it.

``Everything is going to be fine,'' William said, as he cupped it in his hand, seeing for a second his old companion splayed out on the floor, his chewed, defeated toys within paws' reach. He looked outside, saw the figure of his wife, standing above her garden, gloves dirty, pink bandanna in her hair, waving to him and smiling.

He looked again, and they were gone.

``Either way...''

There, he sat, serene, watching the birds outside, chittering among themselves, pecking away at seeds fallen from the trees, strewn about the yard.

``...everything is going to be fine.''

Then he saw them again.

Emily.

Gretzky.

Patiently, happily waiting for him. Under the cool shade of a willow tree. Its branches dancing softly in the early summer breeze.

Everything is going to be fine.

ELEVEN

"Geez, remember when you were that little?"

Nick motioned out the window, towards the kids outside, frolicking and giggling, as Gianna sat down, sighing and looking over her shoulder, smiling.

"It seems ages ago," she said.

"For me too," he said. "Sometimes. But then, other times, something will bring back a memory and the stories are still so fresh in my mind, and the minute details of them still seem so real, it's like I can't believe it was that long ago."

They both watched the kids running, smiling.

"What are they playing?" Gianna said.

"Marco Polo."

"Isn't that supposed to be a pool game? I don't remember ever playing it in a parking lot."

"I don't know. I guess when you're a kid, you don't really think about those things. You just kinda go where your heart and your imagination take you."

"Yeah," she said.

She took a drink. Looked back.

"Hmm?"

She looked back at him. He looked back at her.

"What?" she said.

"What what?" he laughed. "You seem deep in thought."

"I was thinking of Marco Polo," she said.

"Oh, sorry, my mistake," he said.

She smiled.

"Actually, it was kind of deep."

"Really? How so?"

"I don't know, just thinking of the differences between being a kid and being an adult."

"Like…"

"Oh, all sorts of things," she said.

"So what you're saying is that you were thinking about how lucky you are to be old enough to buy booze and fireworks?" he said.

"Yes, that's exactly it," she said. "While voting. And being able to drive a car to do all of them."

"See, that's what I figured," he said.

They sat in silence, for a few moments, both looking at the kids, carefree at play. This was their fifth or sixth date, maybe the fourth, all depending on how you counted it, and if you counted the first couple times they hung out, or the first time they met when they were all hanging out with a group of friends, playing softball. That random meeting. The second was less so, as a smaller group of friends got together, inviting both of them, sort of a matchmaking expedition to see if there was something there.

There was.

And that led to their first, official, duo date, if there had to be such a designation. So maybe this was their fourth. Counting the first couple times, they'd known each other about seven weeks, almost two months. But it seemed longer, in the best ways, and in the past few weeks, there hadn't been a day when they hadn't talked or texted, just random stuff, sending jokes or amusing observations. Nothing really heavy. Just sharing the randomness of life.

"I don't know," she said, breaking the pause. "I guess just thinking about, you know, other adult stuff."

"Like?

"Just, you know."

He laughed. "Well, actually, I don't, which is why I'm asking."

"Relationships, if you must know," she said. "Dating."

"What about it?"

"I guess, ya see, this is why dating is so strange to me," Gianna said. "It both plays to my strength, and my weakness."

"Uh huh," Nick said. "How so?"

"I don't know," she said, and she looked around. His eyes followed hers, curious.

The diner was like something out of an Edward Hopper painting. Wonderfully archaic, innocent and charming. It had been like this as long as Nick could remember. His grandfather started taking him here when he was a kid no larger than those outside, sitting him up at the lunch counter and getting him chocolate malts and patty melts while the grandpas sat around with their coffee and eggs and hash browns and corned beef hash and steaks and talked about the good old days and the not so good old days and the war and their wives and their kids and grandkids, and the way things should be and the way things were.

"Sure you do," he said, smiling, "otherwise you wouldn't have brought it up."

"Ha. Ha." She smirked and took a long drink of iced tea.

If only it was as easy as the first or second date, she thought, when distance was easier, when there were more barriers readily in place. If only it was as easy as being a kid again. We could just fly on and follow impulse, and then blame it on being kids. But as much as she was a free spirit, as much as it seemed as though she didn't need to worry about the growing bond between her and Nick, as much as she was pretty certain, her doubt still gripped her. She remained haunted by goodbyes past, and even worse, over-analysis of where the farewells might have begun, paths taken early on that led nowhere.

She'd started off well, her first few relationships through her teens and twenties mostly ending because they were both young, and timing was off, they wanted different things and went in different directions.

He wanted to settle down and have kids, she wasn't ready to yet.

He got a job and moved away, she was happy where she was at.

She went to grad school and moved away, he was happy where he was at.

That sort of thing. The kind where it hurts, but you know it's for the best and you sincerely do remain friends rather than just saying it with no true intention.

But then there were those of more recent vintage, as she had a wild stretch in her late twenties where there was a consistent string of two-faced liars and assholes, ending in her early thirties with her engagement to the one that topped them all -- a fiancé who seemed perfect at first, but was anything but.

The engagement became a long cohabitation rather than a prelude to a quick wedding. It was a three-year prelude to nothing. Well, not exactly, nothing. She did accumulate plenty of debt in paying for the both of them as he crashed from job to job. And it became her prelude to the breakup that really put her on guard, put her in that suspicious place of having to keep a little distance when dating people, and even worse, that place where she started to doubt her own judgement.

And it all began with the kind gesture of leaving work early to surprise him with dinner to break up the monotony of a month of long nights at work. Instead of having the intended effect, it introduced her to an image she still couldn't completely shake. Two naked bodies scrambling for clothing, pathetically reaching to cover their shame, in a bed and an apartment she was paying for. What a cliché, she still thought, but then again, in all clichés was a well-worn truth. A sad, well-worn truth.

She tried to chalk it up to any number of things, most notably it being him and not her, but it was too late and Eden was decimated, at least for Gianna, paved over and replaced with a couple of short, safe and benign mini-mall relationships. Uninspired, but at least easier to close.

And then, deciding solitude preferable to settling, almost a year alone.

Until now.

Until Nick.

From the minute she saw him, from the minute they talked, she felt that familiar flutter, that rush, that hurricane of the heart. That feeling, like you've already got a connection, like you're meeting someone you've already known in a previous life and there's something inside of you drawing you back to them, almost like you knew you were going to see them again, but you didn't know when, and there's something inside of you that's excited about finally finding them.

But, as she got to know him, she got beyond that smash of infatuation, lust and attraction, that playful banter and goofy back-and-forth, and began to feel a tug of the mind as well. She kept her distance, or, at least tried to, but he was so laid back, so calm, so nurturing, so real, not just with her but with the people around him. She looked for signs, looked for cracks, and had to try to find anything beyond the banal. He was just a nice guy. The kind of guy girls normally overlook or take for granted.

Especially when they're young. Or immature. Which is probably why, with both of them in their thirties, she found him single and burned, the same way she had been.

But, still, as much as she wanted to believe, as much as she wanted to give in, she couldn't.

She couldn't.

Okay, she thought, maybe a little.

``Initially, dating plays to my strength," she said. ``You need to be outgoing and talkative on a date to make it work. You have to have the courage to step forward and throw yourself into conversation with a complete stranger, in order to glean anything about them. Not just in what they say, but in what they don't say, and how they say or don't say it. Or if they even relate to you at all. You can tell a lot by body language."

Nick self-consciously checked his posture in the booth. She shot him a look and rolled her eyes.

``Your body language is just fine," she said. ``You're relaxed, but leaning forward and engaged, and your facial expression connotes interest. Not to mention the fact that you're involved actively in the conversation and not staring at the waitress's legs or looking over my shoulder at the girl walking in the door."

``There's a girl walking in the door?" he asked.

``I can see her in the window behind you."

``I didn't notice."

``Don't push it," she laughed.

"Seriously. I wasn't paying attention to the door. Don't worry though," Nick said. "I think she's only here to buy booze and fireworks."

"And get her drivers license," she added.

"And to register to vote," he returned.

"Of course," she said, raising her eyebrow. "But wait, I thought you said you weren't paying attention to her?"

For a second Nick thought of saying what really passed through his mind at that moment. Which was, ``Why would I want to waste any time looking at anyone else other than you? When you're not around, I can't wait to see you again, to hear you talk and joke and laugh and to just wander and explore you, like some vast hidden realm, and I hope to God that in some way you feel that way too."

But instead, he said...

"Well, once you pointed her out, I wanted to make sure she was leaving some fireworks for the rest of us."

"Nice save."

"Thanks."

``Anyway," Gianna took a sip of her tea. ``Mmm. That's good."

She took another sip.

``Boy, must be really good," Nick said, smiling.

``I'm stalling," she said, buoyant.

"You don't say," Nick laughed.

``Anyway, dating," she smiled with a little laugh, "it plays to my strengths initially because I'm an outgoing person. I'm interested in people and it's fun to make conversation. It's pretty easy. And that's what you want at first, the ability to make quick chatter to establish a bond."

"Ideally, yeah."

``But then, that openness works against you as you start to get into dating someone, when you actually start to discover things about them and you start to like them and you want to know more," she said. ``When you're in that nebulous state between dating and quote-unquote official exclusive relationship, when things could go either way and you're not quite sure where you're gonna go.'"

``So why don't you just take a chance and find out?" he asked, with a mischievous grin.

``Okay," she said, smiling, "So, hypothetically, say you have two people who are dating, both of whom have the goal to get into a relationship, in a general, hypothetical sense."

``Of course," he said, returning her grin. ``We're dealing completely hypothetical here."

``Of course," she said, smiling.

``So, I should, like, pretend you're talking about, say, Bert and Ernie from `Sesame Street.'"

``Nah, it couldn't be Bert and Ernie," Gianna said. ``They live together. They've been together for a couple for years."

``Okay, then Lady Elaine Fairchild and X the Owl from `Mr. Rogers,'" he said.

``Okay, yeah, they've definitely hooked up a few times, the sexual chemistry there is obviously scalding," Gianna said.

``That's why they call him X," Nick said. ``It would've been triple-X, but the censors toned it down."

``Because of his previous career in bird porn."

``Yes, it was quite scandalous. Which brings us back to Big Bird. No irony in that name."

``So I've heard."

``And seen," he said, ``be honest."

``Yeah, you caught me, I can't get enough bird porn," she said.

``I kinda figured you for that," he said. "Good thing you're old enough to buy it."

She rolled her eyes. ``Okay, back on topic...'' she smiled.

``Okay,'' he said, ``so Lady Elaine and X have been out on a couple of dates.''

``Eeew,'' she said. ``This really is hypothetical. I don't fancy myself being Lady Elaine Fairchild.''

``You and you alone,'' Nick said. ``Personally, that's what I do most Friday nights. Or should I say, King Friday nights.''

``TMI.''

``Huh?''

``Too much information,'' she said.

"Or maybe just enough," he raised an eyebrow.

"Maybe," she said, "I'll leave you with a cliffhanger there. To be continued."

``So, anyway, these hypothetical people, who aren't us, and aren't Lady Elaine and X, have been out on a couple of dates,'' he said.

``And they both hit it off,'' she said, ``and if, deep down, they see potential there, then why hide it?''

"Because one of them is afraid of sharing the sordid truth about their bird fetish?"

"Possibly," she said, "but what if the other also has the same fetish unbeknownst to the first person, and they don't even know it yet?"

"Wow, they sound like a terrific couple!" he said. "Plenty of fireworks. And liquor. And voting."

She rolled her eyes and took a drink.

He smiled.

"Don't worry about it," he said. "Someone once said to me, 'Don't waste time worrying about things you may never have to worry about, because, most of the time, you don't. Most of the time, everything's going to be fine.' And in regard to any relationships, concentrate on being happy in the present, because if you put enough great days in the present together, the future kinda takes care of itself."

"That's a great fortune cookie," she said.

"Actually, I got it from Oprah."

"She gave it to you personally?"

"Yeah," he said. "We're tight."

She plopped her elbows on the table and sighed, deflated, sticking out her tongue at him playfully, and then smiling widely.

Outside, the kids could be heard, louder.

"Marco!"

"Polo!"

He looked out the window, amused. "Man, they're really getting into it out there!"

"Yeah," she said, raising an eyebrow and smirking. "But aside from that distraction, I think you know what I'm saying."

He lifted his coffee cup up, slowly, and began to take a drink.

And as he did, a tsunami of thoughts flooded dangerously and excitedly through his head.

``Well, I think I have an idea," he imagined himself saying to her, ``you know how it is when you meet someone and you just click together. You first see them and you think...

```Wow.'

``And you're just stunned by them. And then you start talking to them and you can't believe you're actually there, actually having a conversation like this because it's so good and it's going so well.

``You bring out that mental checklist of things you look for, and before you know it, the boxes of the first page are filled with red checks, and so you flip it over and start to fill in the next page and before you know it, you feel closer and closer to this person.
```

``But then, you remember you can't, not yet, because you don't know if this person's checklist is even close to full, or if she even has the red pen out, or if she's even interested in you at all.

``So the walls and the guards kick in, and eventually you get to the end of the date, but your guard isn't up enough for you to not want to ask to see them again. And, fortunately, they say yes and you're ecstatic, you're buzzing, you're completely high.

``But then you start to think about it and the reality sets in that you're already starting to become invested, however slightly, and it gives you a little pause that someone has that power over you to make you happy, and you get a little scared because of it. But it feels so good and you realize that it's such a short-lived thing and it feels so amazing so you don't want to let it pass you by. It's been a while since you felt that way so you think that it's okay and you let it sail.

``And then you get a couple dates in, and you're thinking, `This is it, this is make or break time. Anyone can have a great first couple dates, anyone can get through the generalities.'

``But then you start to think about your conversations and you realize that the things you had in common weren't just generalities, they were specifics. It wasn't just like, `Hey, you like Italian food, me too!' It was an array of specific things that determine you, and who you really are, and the type of person you like, and the type of person you'd like to be with.

"But you discount that and you put that aside, because you think of previous relationships that didn't work out, that also started great, and you think that there are a lot of other single people out there and that you can find someone else, and that one person not being interested in you isn't the end of the world.

"And so, in your mind, it's kind of like you've already prepared yourself for the worst, so you're relaxed. And isn't it kind of sick that you relax yourself by thinking the worst is going to occur so you're already prepared for it? But it works, so you ride with it.

"And then you start to really click, again, and again, and so when you see her again each time it's those butterflies and that 'Wow' feeling again but this time it's even more intense and then you go do something and you spend some more time together and you talk some more and then before you know it the restaurant or whatever is closing and you can't believe that it's been four hours you've been there talking together because it doesn't feel like any time has passed at all, and there's still so much you want to say, so much you want to see, so much you want to do with this person, this wonderful being that you've just discovered but seen so little of. What you've seen is so amazing and beautiful that you can't wait to see the rest. You can't wait to feel this way again, to feel like there's this person out there, this person who you didn't even know existed who has been on this planet that you have this tentative incredible link with now. It's like a spider web, so strong yet so fragile, and all that potential that was there is now finally maybe going to take shape and change your lives forever.

"And now when you kiss, it's different, it's like something happens and you're not just two people touching skin and feeling a tingle anymore, it's like you're starting to feel like you're floating in space. You lose yourself a little, you lose yourself in the moment and you're not self-conscious at all, you're just gliding along on this silver wave that overtakes you and gently washes you into one another where you commingle and create this new thing that wasn't there before, and it's the seed of what you could be, if only you could overcome that fear and realize that she's just a person, just like you, and that maybe, just maybe, she's feeling the same way, just like you, and she's afraid and tired and wary and timid but deep down she's hopeful.

``Hopeful. And that's why she's with you in the first place. That's why she's kissing you. That's why she wants to go out with you again. She's hopeful that you won't be like all the rest, and that maybe, just maybe, this time the love songs will all start to make sense and that maybe all the people prior to this one were just there to lead you up to this moment with this one person. And that, hell, even if they weren't, who cares? You're with this person now and all the rest doesn't matter as long as things still keep going in this way, as long as this feeling doesn't stop, and you don't want it to stop, you want it to keep growing and growing and just getting stronger and stronger because it's the best damn thing you've felt in so long, and the best thing about it is that you feel like you're sharing it with someone else who you think is just so . . . cool, is just so . . . true."

Nick put his empty coffee cup down, sighed, and for another moment he thought about how quickly those thoughts had leapt into his head, as if he had very little control over them at all. And for a moment he was surprised that even after all he'd been through, even after all the times he'd been disappointed, he could still feel that way. And so, he considered saying them, but very quickly he knew that there was no way those thoughts could leave his head. At least not for a good long while.

So, he looked up at Gianna, and said...

"Yeah, I do think I know what you're saying, and just to let you know, I'm really glad you've entered my life. I think you're an incredible person, you're smart and funny and beautiful and sexy and cool, and I hope you're not leaving any time soon."

She looked up at him, raised an eyebrow and smiled.

"Ditto."

He broke out in laughter.

"I'm kidding! I'm kidding!" she said.

"I guess it's better than, 'I know,'" he said.

"Yeah," she said. "I could've Soloed you."

"I should've Soloed you!" he said.

"Hey, hey, hey," she said. "You probably thought about it. It took you fifteen seconds of silence to come up with that."

"Sorta," he laughed. "That's the Cliff's Notes version."

Gianna remained silent, looking at him, her face, wide and bright, her eyes gold in the light from the sun fading outside, her lips parted for a caress of breath, in a slight smile.

"Well," she said. "I hope that someday you let me read the whole novel. And I promise, I won't Solo you. If you really must know, and I guess you must, I feel the same way. I really do. I think you're great. You're smart and you're funny and you're kind and you're handsome and you're sexy and and I love being with you, and I hope you stick around a while, because I want you to."

He laughed. "Good to know."

They looked at each other, silent, smiling.

"Maybe," she said.

They laughed.

And then she leaned over the table to him, and he met her halfway, and she looked into his eyes, and he kissed her.

Again.

And again.

And again.

And the kids outside giggled and yelled.

"Marco!"

"Polo!"

TWELVE

They walked from the stark, humid dusk of city sounds outside into a cluttered room of low, cool, artificial light, the bells of the opening door chiming as a closing eye of crimson and gold shut behind them. Once inside, the velvet darkness of the room revealed a world in miniature, a fantasy diorama of times past freckled by gentle illumination.

The sounds of model trains going through ornate clay and plaster mountain tunnels accompanied small wisps of smoke, haloing the flecks of fading neon and shrunken business signs in red, white and blue, yellow, silver and green.

The boy gasped in wonder.

The man had seen it before, smiled in recognition, and slowly found his way to the counter.

"Wow, cool," the boy said as his eyes devoured the diorama enveloping the small trains rolling along the tracks, tiny lights flickering on and off, old Christmas lights strung above the papier mache landscapes of mountains and mines, rivers and lakes, miniscule cities and towns that lived and died at the whims of their creators every few months.

"Yeah," a man's voice, deep and craggy as the mountain dioramas, said. "It's different with the lights down. You see things you otherwise might not. Causes you to focus more."

"Hey, I'm gonna turn the lights back on, I gotta customer," another gravelly voiced man said as he moved to the counter. "Hey, I'm Walt. How can I help you?"

The lights flicked on, revealing the massive sprawl of miniature train depots and small town relics, snaking around one side of the collectibles shop, surrounded by shelves of comics, records, model vehicles, autographed pictures and odd trinkets, baubles and myriad geek currency.

"Hey, Ben, sorry, couldn't see ya in the dark," Walt said, looking at the man before him at the counter. "And, guess I haven't seen ya in a while."

"Yeah," Ben said. "I've been busy. Things been going well?"

"Yeah, sure, same old same old."

"Hey Dad, can I look around?" the boy said.

"Yeah, Nick, just stay where I can see you."

Nick strolled off, his eyes filling with new worlds.

"Boy, he's gettin' big," Walt said. "But, like I said, been a while."

"Yeah."

"Lookin' for anything in particular? I've gotten a lot of new stuff in since you've been by."

"Well," Ben said. "I'm actually looking to sell."

"Sell?"

"Yeah."

"Whatcha got?"

Ben lifted two large boxes onto the counter.

Packed with vinyl records.

"Whoh."

"Yeah."

"Seriously?"

"Yup."

Walt started flipping through, stopped at one and looked up at him.

"You're selling this?"

"Yeah," Ben said, as the little boy beelined over to him, hugging him, Ben wrapping his arm around his son.

"Can I look at those comics over there?" Nick said.

"Yeah, sure."

"Can I get one?"

"Sure, pal."

Walt kept flipping through the records. Stopping again, and again, and again.

"Half of these are autographed."

"Yeah."

"They're all legit?"

"I've still got a lot of the video from when I interviewed 'em, want to see it to make sure?"

"Nah, I believe you," Walt said, taking one out and admiring it. "Can't say I'd give everyone the benefit of the doubt, but I'm pretty sure I can trust you."

"Good to know." Ben chuckled.

Walt looked hard at Ben. "You really want to sell these? You're sure?"

"Yeah."

"Want store credit? Gettin' into somethin' else?"

"No, cash."

"Ya know, ya get more in credit."

"Yeah, but what I need you don't have here," Ben chuckled. "Unless you've started carrying diapers and formula."

Walt smiled.

"Not that I'm aware of."

Walt sighed. "Okay, let me take a look at 'em and check the guides. Give me a few minutes."

"Sounds good," Ben said, looking around and finding Nick, then reaching into his pocket and pulling out a black-and-silver rectangle camera and raising it at him.

"Nick, say cheese."

The little boy smiled halfheartedly, then stuck out his tongue, and then, finally, gave his Dad a huge toothy smile as the flash popped.

"Let me take a couple more."

Nick continued to smile, standing upright near the stacks of comics and cards he'd been perusing, one hand on a box of Fantastic Fours.

"Thanks, pal," Ben said, putting the camera away. "Love you."

"Love you too."

Walt smiled, continued to flip through the albums and thumb, deliberately, through the plump price guide.

"I'm gonna have some empty shelf space," Ben smirked, "so I'm gonna need some pictures to fill it."

"Guess so," Walt said, distracted.

A younger man with long hair and a beat-up leather jacket hovered behind them, nosing over the second box.

"Hey man, mind if I?"

"Fine with me," Ben said. "Walt?"

"If you want to buy 'em direct from him, I'll look the other way," Walt said. "Just this once."

"Thanks Walt."

"Well, I treat my regulars right. Even if they're not regulars anymore. Never know, they might be again."

"Never know."

"Yeah, things change, ya know," Walt said, a bit melancholy. "It's like I always say to these kids. They're always sayin' how life is short and all that. Life ain't short. Life is long. It just seems short when you've only been here a short time. Ya can't see how long it's gonna be 'til ya been there."

"That's true," Ben said.

"Very true," the younger man added, looking up.

The younger man pulled a half dozen of the records gingerly from the box, looked them over, and pulled a couple of bills from his ratty brown wallet.

"Would you be willing to take this for these?"

"Fair enough," Ben smiled, making the exchange.

The man smiled back, saluted at Walt and Ben, and walked out as Walt began looking through the boxes again.

"You bought most of these here, didn't you?" he said to Ben.

"Well, yeah. Most of the autographed copies I got myself, but there were a few I picked up from you. Once upon a time."

Walt looked at a scrawl over a pristine white sleeve.

"I know you didn't get this from me," he said. "Is that really?"

"Yeah."

"How'd you get it?"

"Interviewed him a few years ago, when he was on tour, after they broke up. Solo."

Walt raised his eyebrows and his forehead scrunched, impressed.

One of the men from the railway club, a paunchy, joyful, middle-aged guy with a red face and thin silver glasses, had been hovering around the counter.

"Your wife makin' you sell those?" he smiled, conspiratorily.

"No," Ben said. "Just, don't need 'em anymore. Or, actually, just need other things more."

"Yeah," the man said, running a hand over his buzz cut. "My wife wanted me to sell a whole bunch of my stuff when we got married, and I sold some of it, but not all. And that turned out to be a good thing, because it sure as hell lasted a lot longer than she did."

Walt scowled at the man. "Jimmy, there were bananas lasted longer than you and Jean."

The three laughed.

"Yeah," Jimmy said, "That's the way it goes. That's why I said I'm never changin' again for anyone, any woman. That's the difference between a woman and my things. Your things never disappoint you, they never change."

"Really?" Walt reached to a shelf, then turned and tossed a broken model airplane onto the counter. "That sure did. Damn thing busted first week I had it, been tryin' to fix the damn thing ever since and can't get it right."

Jimmy laughed, then motioned to the small group of middle-aged men collecting their things behind him.

"Well Walt, we're headin' out," he said. "You gonna meet us at the Knights later?"

"Yeah, I'll be down there in an hour or two."

"Sounds good."

He nodded to Ben, smiled at Walt and left.

Walt got out a pad of paper and began to write down some figures. He exhaled heavily, looked down, and slid the paper over to Ben.

"How's that? For everything."

Ben looked down, stared at it for a few seconds and looked back up.

"Sounds good to me."

"Deal," Walt reached out and shook Ben's hand.

"I'll even throw in a couple comics for your boy," Walt said, motioning towards Nick. "Just as long as they're not any of the real expensive ones."

Ben chuckled. "Fair enough."

Walt nodded, then turned and grabbed a large carbon-and-yellow receipt pad.

"I just need your driver's license," Walt said, as Ben reached for his wallet. "I know who you are and all, I just need the numbers and info and stuff. This much new inventory, gotta keep the records, you know. Pain in the ass."

Ben put the card on the counter.

Walt studied it for a few seconds.

"William?"

He looked up at Ben.

"Yeah. That's my real name," Ben said. "My real first name, that is."

"Hmmm." Walt looked back down, started writing on the pad. "William... Benjamin... Barstow..."

He looked back up at Ben.

"Why'd you go by your middle name?"

"It was a TV thing. Alliteration. Sounds better. Ben Barstow. William Barstow. B.B. Sounds better, catchier, I guess. A producer talked me into it when I was younger."

"Why didn't ya just go by Bill? That has a B too."

"Never really thought of it," Ben said. "I guess neither did the producer either because he came up with Ben. I liked it. It is still my name. So it's not like I had a problem changing it."

"Ever think of changing it back?" Walt said. "Now that you're not on TV?"

"Funny you mention that, actually I have," Ben said. "I was just filling out some paperwork and had to write my legal name down a couple times and got to thinking about that."

"What kinda paperwork? You're not gettin' a divorce too, are ya?"

"No. Emily and I just had another baby."

"Well, congratulations," Walt said.

"Thanks."

"Boy or girl?"

"Boy."

"Two boys now."

"Yeah."

"That's trouble," Walt winked.

"We'll see."

"What's his name? The new guy?"

"Simon."

Walt looked up. "Simon. That's a name you don't hear every day. How'd you come up with it?"

"Emily did."

"Where'd she get it? Family name?"

"The Bible, actually. He was one of the disciples. And it means 'to listen to, to be heard.'"

"Hmm."

"Kind of a private thing," Ben said, looking down.

Walt raised his hand as if to wipe away any imposition and gave Ben a nod. He scribbled a few last lines on the paper and handed it to Ben to sign.

"Wish I could give you more," Walt said as Ben looped a large, practiced scrawl onto the bottom line.

"Don't worry about it, this is fine," Ben said.

"If it was just a couple years back, I could've..."

"Well, if it was just a couple years back, I might not be here selling these either," Ben said, with a slight smile.

"Things are tough all over," Walt said, peeling out bills and placing them on the counter. "I know what ya mean."

He looked out over the shop.

"I don't know how much longer I'm gonna be doin' this," he said. "My kid just got back from the Navy and can't find anything. Like a lotta other kids his age. I'm thinkin' of bringin' him on here, gettin' him ready to take over if he wants to."

"What will you do?"

"What did I do before here?" the man chuckled with a crooked smile. "Something. I'm sure I'll find something to entertain me and occupy my time."

"I'm sure you will," Ben said, as Nick ran towards him with a couple of comics.

Ben held the comics up for Walt.

"Oh, those are fine," Walt said, smiling at the boy. "You have fun readin' 'em."

"Thanks mister."

Ben and Nick turned to leave. "We'll see ya later, Walt."

"Don't be a stranger," Walt said. "Even if ya aren't buyin' or sellin', just stop in to say hi from time to time. We do the railroad thing for the kids on weekends sometimes and my son's gonna be doin' some more comics stuff. He's an artist. Might do caricatures or something."

"I'll do that," Ben said, nodding. "Thanks Walt. Take care."

"You too."

As they walked towards the door, another man, in a suit and tie, walked in, looked around the store, stopped, looked at Ben and did a double take.

"Ben Barstow?"

"Yeah," Ben said.

"I watch you all the time," he said. "It's great to finally meet you."

"Nice to meet you too, uh…"

"Rafe!"

"Good to meet you, Rafe."

"I really like your work, like I said, the wife and I watch you all the time."

"Thanks."

"You're still on 7, right?"

"Well, actually," Ben said, "no."

"Wow, wait, did you change stations?"

"Well, no, actually, I got fired a while ago."

"You're not on TV anymore?"

"Nah, I haven't been on for over a year now."

"Too bad," Rafe said. "Yeah, like I said, my wife and I used to watch you all the time. We really liked you."

"Thanks."

"So what are you doing now?"

"Well, actually, I just started selling insurance."

"Really? Huh. Well," Rafe said. "Maybe I'll look you up. We've been talking about shopping around for a new agency maybe, we'll look you up. Are you in the book?"

"Yeah. Will be."

"Well, great," Rafe said. "Well, uh, I'll look you up and give you a call."

"Sounds good," Ben said, before pausing, "you know, if you do though, look under 'William Barstow.' Not 'Ben.'"

William turned and opened the door for his son, the last rays of the fading day cracking into the shop, framing their shadows long and hazy, over the world in miniature.

"Okay, William, I guess, since you're not," Rafe smiled, nervously attempting to copy Ben's baritone, "'Ben Barstow' anymore."

"Oh, I'll always be Ben Barstow," William said. "That's who I was, for a long time.

"But," William said, leaning slowly out the door, as Nick walked out with his head buried in a comic, "I guess what's more important is who I am now and who I'm going to be."

And the door closed behind them, the shadows faded, and the man and boy walked off, leaving the first few night moths, beating themselves into the lights just outside the door, in their wake.

THIRTEEN

"You know you're adopted, don't you?"

The boy looked smugly at the girl.

She rolled her eyes at him.

"You know your real parents are Ronald McDonald and the Grimace, and one day, when I was very little, Mom and Dad, well, my Mom and Dad, my real Mom and Dad, your adoptive parents, we were all at McDonald's and we saw the Grimace and Ronald McDonald and they were outside fighting – I think it had something to do with the Grimace having an affair with Mayor McCheese or something like that – and they offered us a whole bunch of McDonald's gift certificates and stuff if we'd take you off their hands."

"You don't say."

"No, I do say, because it's the truth," the boy said, earnestly. "And so for the first four or five years of your life you ate nothing but Big Macs and McFlurries and so did we, and that's why Mom, well, my Mom, your adoptive mother, has that big collection of collector's glasses, but, if you look really hard, you'll notice that the one for the Grimace is just slightly smaller than all the rest. I think it's a jealousy thing, just to kind of diminish the competition or something. It might be Freudian."

"You don't even know what Freudian means."

"I know that you were born with a vestigial bun, I know that, and that it had to be surgically removed."

"Do I even have to dignify this with a reply?"

"No, you can continue living in denial if you want, I don't mind. I just figured you might want to know before you turn 18 and your hair starts turning bright red and your skin goes a dark purple, which, if you really look in the mirror, it seems to already be turning..."

The girl looked to the front seat at her aunt and uncle.

"Are we there yet?"

"No, not yet," Nick said.

Gianna looked at him and then glanced sideways at the back seat and stifled a laugh.

"Are you sure you want to do this?" Nick said.

"Are you?"

"Yeah, it'll be fun," he said. "The kids'll enjoy it and I'm sure Faith and Hector will enjoy the time to themselves."

"That's true," she said. "I'm sure they will. Probably rearrange their McDonald's collectors' cups."

"Right," Nick said, with a laugh. "And it'll be good for us, I mean, you never know, the agency could end up matching us with an older child or two older children, and we'll be better prepared to discuss that possibility if we have more experience with older kids."

"That is true as well," she said, smiling. "You never know."

"And it might be good experience," he said, dryly, "dealing with a child that's already been adopted."

"Yes," Gianna said, with mock seriousness. "Especially if we end up with the Hamburglar's child with Wendy or something like that."

They drove past a quick cropping of signs, huge florescent weeds against the waves of grassland.

"About another half hour or so and we'll stop," Nick said.

"What did that sign say?" Luis yelled from the back seat.

"It said there's a rest area about a half hour away, we'll stop there."

"No, not that one, the other one."

"What other one?"

"The other one. Did that actually say 'No Hitchhiking?'"

"Yeah, I guess it did. Must be an old sign. You don't usually see a lot of hitchhikers."

"Well, don't pick any up, especially if they have a hook for a hand," Luis said.

"I'll take that under advisement," Nick said.

"Please do," Luis said.

There was a silence for a few seconds.

"And don't pull over on the side of the road either," Luis added.

"Why not?" Nick said.

"Just in case there are any invisible hitchhikers, hitchhiking that might jump into our car."

"I tend to doubt it, but I also tend to doubt I'll be stopping on the side of the road either, so I wouldn't worry about it too much, Luis."

"Okay, just making sure."

"Your diligence is always appreciated."

"Not always," Luis said.

Simone guffawed.

"What are you laughing at?"

"Invisible hitchhikers."

"There are invisible hitchhikers."

"No there aren't."

"Yes there are."

"Oh, give me a break."

Luis pouted for a few seconds.

"Speaking of invisible hitchhikers," Luis said, "did I also mention that your real brother is Casper the Friendly Ghost?"

"Good to know," Simone said, keeping her eyes on her book.

They drove on for another fifteen minutes. It was quiet. Too quiet.

"How are you guys doing back there?" Nick looked into the rearview mirror.

"Fine," Luis said. "Simone was just telling me of her great love for Ukiah McOatstein."

"Ukiah McOatstein?" Nick said. "Who's that?"

"The Quaker Oats guy."

"Oh," Nick made a face to Gianna. "Okay."

Gianna giggled.

"Again, you sure you want to do this?"

Nick laughed.

"I am not in love with the Quaker Oats guy," Simone protested without looking up from her book.

"Ukiah McOatstein," Luis said, sitting on his hands and rocking slightly. "You know his name. You can say it. I know it probably melts your heart a little just to utter those beautiful, melodic syllables but I think if you center yourself you can actually say it loud and proud."

"Shut up."

"Well, if you shut up you can't say it. C'mon, Ukiah McOatstein. You should know it quite well, you've whispered it longingly thousands of times."

"Shut up."

"You've got it tattooed on your bum."

"Shut... since when are you British? Bum. You're a giant dork."

"And you, my youngest sister, are a giant lover of Ukiah McOatstein."

"One, I'm your only sister, and two, I'm ignoring you."

Simone continued reading while Luis fidgeted, clicking a pen in and out, on and off, before looking at her mischievously.

Slowly, he began to move his hands around her, without touching, but just barely, as if she had a force field surrounding her. He moved ever closer to her without touching her, taunting her. She rolled her eyes and ignored him.

Slowly, he started to poke her arm.

She ignored him.

He kept poking, slowly, slowly, then increasing a little faster and faster and faster until...

She turned to him and made a fist.

He backed off.

He reached for his notebook and pen and started writing in it.

"Captain's Log," Luis formally began, as he wrote, "Female subject responds to 36 pokes with animosity and clenched fist. The test subject seems distressed and confused. I will continue observations and experiments with this obviously low-level primate."

Luis put the notebook down.

He began making a popping sound with his mouth. Not loud enough for the adults in the front seat to hear, but close enough to Simone for her to get it in her ear loud and clear.

She ignored him.

He began grinding his teeth.

She ignored him.

He started making squeaking fart noises.

She shoved him.

"Nick, Gianna! Simone shoved me!"

"Huh! Well he poked me first, and then he was..."

"Guys!" Nick said in a deep voice. "Calm it down. Act your ages."

"Ok, but we're only..." Luis began.

"Act more mature than your ages!" Nick clipped in.

Both of them went silent in the back seat.

Simone went back to reading.

Luis went back to rocking back and forth, before grabbing his notebook and writing again, reciting his scribbling out loud.

"Stinky poo-butt smelling primate subject responds to playful heckling with stinky poo-butt tattling, which results in science project being temporarily delayed for potential lack of allowance funding."

The two of them sat silent for a few moments. Simone continuing to read, Luis continuing to look at her and make odd faces.

"How much longer?" Luis asked.

"Not too much, only an hour or so," Nick said. "There's a rest area up here, we'll stop in a few minutes to get some snacks and take a break."

"Okay, cool," Luis said.

Gianna looked back at the kids as Simone continued reading her book and Luis looked out the window. Then she looked at Nick.

They'd been together for a little over five years total now, married for almost two of them. While so many of her friends had left their marriages, invariably with some vague complaint of them lacking some element of soap opera-level roller coaster thrills, Gianna found herself even more attracted to Nick because he was one of the most drama-free people she'd ever met. Not to say he wasn't exciting and fun and impulsive and open to new things, because he was. But he was also responsible and reasonable and laid back.

Life was unpredictable enough. He was the rock she could always count on. No matter what happened, no matter what came his way, her way, not much bothered him. He'd just surf the wave. There was none of the drama, none of the unpredictability, none of the mood swings that her friends seemed to find so compelling in their relationships, maybe just to give them something to talk about, something to complain about.

She remembered something someone once told her, "Find meaning within yourself and you won't seek it elsewhere." And the way she looked at it, she had found meaning in her own life before she met Nick. She wasn't with him because she needed to be, she was with him because she wanted to be. She could live without him, because she had before. But she preferred to live with him in her life, because it made her life better, and his, that they were together. That difference made all the difference.

As Nick and Gianna were sitting at home watching movies, making fun of the improbability of a romantic comedy, their friends were out vainly trying to make one happen for themselves and, minus clever editors and script doctors, failing miserably. When Nick was calling her on the regular every afternoon to check in and see what they wanted to do for dinner, her friends were wondering when the guy of the month was going to text, or if he was ever going to. While her friends were seemingly always unsure of where they stood, constantly snooping for clues on whether or not the guy they were with was cheating or whatever, she never worried about that with Nick. She knew he'd been cheated on a few times and it left a mark, to the point where he swore to her that he'd never do that to her, and she trusted him. He never gave her any reason not to.

"You guys are so boring," they'd say of Gianna and Nick.

Gianna was quite happy with that. She'd had enough of the opposite pre-Nick. She liked just living life and enjoying the life they'd made together. Spending time together doing everyday things. Joking around about silly stuff. Spending time with Nick's niece and nephew, and her nephews, being the parents they weren't able to be, yet.

Her parents used to tell her, when you find someone you can do everyday stuff with and be happy, that's the one, because most of life is everyday stuff.

And maybe it was because when she thought of her parents, thought of what she would do if she had one more day with them, she never thought of taking trips or riding roller coasters, she just thought, if she just had more time with them, all she could think of doing would be the little things they used to do, that she took for granted.

She looked down at her wedding ring, fidgeted with it a few seconds and watched the sun bend prisms of color and light within it, changing its look within the same shape.

She looked down at her bag, picked it up, picked through it, thought for a second, then put it down.

Then she looked over at Nick, reached out and held his hand.

He grasped hers, lifted it to his lips and kissed it, and smiled.

In the back seat, the natives became restless again.

"You know, you kinda look like Michael Jackson," Luis began, to his younger sister.

"No, no, you look like Beetlejuice."

"No, you look like Mr. Clean."

"That's it. you look just like Mr. Clean."

Simone continued to ignore him.

"I happened to see you had tuna for lunch," Luis said, cheekily. "Did you know that that tuna you ate, Bumble Bee, is made from crushed bumble bees?"

Nothing.

"Yeah, they take all the fish out and they put the bumble bees in and they crush them up to make them look just like fish. but if you look really closely, you can see their stingers and their yellow and black fur, and once they get into your stomach, if they were pregnant when they got chopped up, then their eggs, which were too small to get chopped up, will come to life in your stomach and hatch and then your stomach will be filled with bumble bees. And they'll be really mad and want to sting your insides and you'll get all swollen up and you'll explode."

"No they don't," Simone said, without looking up from her book.

"Oh yeah," Luis said. "Did I forget to tell you that you were married to Bert from `Sesame Street?' That you're in love with him?"

"No, you failed to mention that."

"And that you're also in love with Elmo and Mr. Hooper and that Ernie is jealous of you because you're married to his best friend and that he's also really mad at you because you're cheating on his best friend with Mr. Hooper?"

Simone began to grit her teeth. Luis smirked.

"Did I tell you that you want to have a lesbian affair with Flo from the Progressive commercials? With Ellen and Flo? That you want to wear her bandana on your head because it's special to you and talk about insurance all the time because you're in love with her and you're a lesbian and you're in love with Ellen and Oprah and Flo?"

Simone began to tap her foot while burying herself deeper in her book.

"And did I tell you that you're also in love with the Quaker Oats guy on the oatmeal box? That you want to have his babies and feed them oatmeal and change their diapers and change his adult diapers and ..."

"Shut up!" Simone snapped.

"That's good," Luis said calmly. "You'll have to learn to speak loudly to him because he's so old."

Simone slammed her book shut and smacked Luis repeatedly across the arm and chest with it, attempting to score a direct hit to the head but instead finding his arms wrapped around it, protecting his flushed, chortling face.

"Hey you guys! Cut it out back there!" Nick said.

Simone stopped, blew a wayward hair off her face, glared at Luis and faked a punch at him, watched him flinch, went back to reading.

Luis picked up his pen and notebook, began writing and quietly reciting his fake journal.

"Girl responds to revelation of her hot, steamy affair with the Quaker Oats man by cruelly punching younger brother. Her volatile reaction thus proves to the world and all the tabloids that the rumors of her and Ukiah McOatstein are irrefutably true once and for all."

Simone put her book down.

But she didn't hit Luis.

She didn't make him flinch.

She didn't do anything.

She just stared straight ahead.

And then, she began to quietly sob.

A sob that began slow and low but quickly ascended into a jiggly, messy whine and a tear drenched cry.

"Ohhh, God!" she wailed.

"It's me, Margaret!" Luis added, laughing.

But she wasn't laughing, and neither were Gianna and Nick.

"Are you okay Simone?" Gianna asked.

"Luis, what did you do?" Nick said.

"I, I, I..." Luis fumbled.

"Don't worry, honey, we're going to stop here," Gianna said, as Nick pulled off at the rest stop.

Luis, perhaps sensing punishment, perhaps feeling remorse, but either way, realizing that the car was going to be stopping soon, quickly leapt in.

"I'm sorry, Simone! I'm sorry! Don't cry."

She sobbed even louder, burying her head in her hands and wringing her hair.

"I'm sorry Simone! You don't love Ukiah McOatstein. You don't love any of those guys. You're not a lesbian with Flo. Don't cry. Would it make you happy if... would it make you feel better if I said I was in love with Ukiah McOatstein?"

Suddenly Simone sat up, perfectly lucid, with a devilish smile on her face, and pointed at him.

"Gotcha! You're in love with Ukiah McOatstein!"

She exploded in laughter.

Luis pouted.

Simone grabbed his pen and opened her book, as if taking notes, while reciting out loud.

"Subject responds to phony tears and sobbing with wimpy girlyman apology and admission of scandalous love affair with Ukiah McOatstein..."

The car stopped.

Nick and Gianna looked to the back seat.

"Simone, why don't you come with me," Gianna said, glancing at Nick. "We'll meet you back here, 'kay?"

Nick and Gianna kissed goodbye, and the two girls got out and walked towards the large, taupe-and-brick '70s style brick rest area.

"Do you have to go?" Nick asked Luis.

"I can wait. We're almost there, right?"

"Yeah, pretty much."

"Ok."

Luis and Nick stayed behind.

"Awww, man!" Luis whined.

"What is it?"

"Look."

His hands were blue with exploded pen ink.

"Hold on a minute."

Nick looked through the car compartments, finding nothing close to a tissue, wipe or cleaning material.

"Hold on, let me see if Aunt Gianna has anything in her purse," he said, reaching down to grab it and beginning to pass through it. "Otherwise, you can just go inside with me and wash them when they get back."

Nick shuffled for a few seconds, and then, stopped.

"Did you find something?" Luis asked.

Nick was quiet.

"Uncle Nick? Did you find something to wipe my hands with?"

Nick regained himself.

"Oh, uh, no, um, you'll have to just go inside. Um, why don't we just get out of the car and you can go in, I'll walk you over there so you don't have to deal with the mess, let's just do it right now."

Luis got out of the car and waited.

"Just start walking, I'll be with you in a minute," Nick said, as Luis began bounding towards the building. Nick followed a few seconds later.

Luis ran in just as Gianna was walking out.

"Whoh!"

"He blew a pen up in his hands."

"Ewww."

"Yeah."

She looked at Nick, then inside.

"So, did you want to get anything quick here, or..."

She looked back at Nick.

"What?"

He gave her a quizzical look.

"What?" she halted.

He looked at her, arched an eyebrow, then, soberly, reached into his pocket, taking out a crumpled brown paper bag, opening it up and pulling out a bright pink cardboard package.

She looked up at him.

"I was looking for something for him to use to clean his hands, and I just happened to find this..." he said, smiling. "What could this be?"

"What does it look like?" she grinned in return.

"Well, obviously... did...you?"

"You dork! I was going to wait until I went to the doctor to make sure! We've been trying for so long and I didn't want to get our hopes up until I could be completely sure..."

He didn't let her finish.

He grabbed her in his arms and held her tight to him and kissed her, again and again and again until he tasted the salt of her tears rolling down her face onto his lips.

Tears of faith.

Tears of joy.

Tears of a new beginning.

A new life.

They were still entwined when the kids walked out.

"Ewww," Luis said.

"Awww," Simone said.

"I noticed they had Funjuns in the vending machine," Luis said. "Is that why you two are so happy?"

Nick and Gianna held each other tight.

Simone noticed the package in Nick's hand.

"Holy cow!" she shrieked. "You guys are gonna have a baby?"

Nick and Gianna leaned apart a bit, both elated, Gianna nodding.

Simone clasped her hands together and grinned.

Luis smiled.

"That's cool," he said. "You know what I think you should name it?"

Nick rolled his eyes.

"We're not naming it Ukiah McOatstein."

Luis shook his head.

"No, I was going to say Luis. You should name him Luis."

"What if it's a her?" Simone added.

"Louisa," he smirked. "Simone."

Nick and Gianna walked hand in hand back to the car, the kids following a few steps behind.

"Geez," Luis said. "Ukiah McOatstein. Hmmph. Who's going to name a kid Ukiah McOatstein?"

He waited until Nick and Gianna got back to kissing and took the opportunity of their distraction to nudge Simone, whispering in her ear.

"Except for you, that is," he said, "because you'd be naming him after his father."

Simone rolled her eyes and smiled.

"Wouldn't I be naming him Bert then?" she said. "Or maybe Mr. Hooper? Or maybe I'd just be having a baby with one of them so that I, and Ellen, and Flo, and Oprah, could adopt, because I'm adopted after all, in which case the baby would have one of our names?"

She laughed.

Luis slanted his eyes mischievously and gave her a tight smile.

"Well played, my adopted sister and daughter of Ronald McDonald and Grimace. Well played."

FOURTEEN

The cafe pinged like an espresso machine, the fizzle and froth of conversations creating a steady buzz.

Almost all the tables were packed. It was a Friday night, just after dusk. Fall. Clear. Just into sweater weather. The promise of new semesters fueling the hum of laptops and discussion.

I was trying my best. Trying my best, slothing halfway through a dark cup of brainpower, scrubbing along lines for a story, a journal, something, just to get things out, in a cheap black spiral notebook.

That's when I saw her.

She wasn't like the other women. That's for sure.

For one thing, she was dressed like she was auditioning for a children's book character.

Wide-brimmed light straw hat. Blue gingham collared shirt with flower appliques shawled around her shoulders over a pink blouse conservatively buttoned to the top. Crisp denim skirt draping down to mid-calf, just over pink socks folded above the ankles to display yipping white dogs sewn on them, and saddle shoes.

Her face was round, sunshiney, with saucer eyes and pink teacup lips. She looked like a Campbell's soup kid, even though her gray bunned hair and grandmotherly demeanor pegged her somewhere in her sixties, at least.

She passed by my table without saying a word. Smiling. Silently smiling.

Then she passed by again.

And again.

Finally she stood at the bar end of the cafe, where it opened up into the bookstore, into the seas of bookshelves and CD and DVD trays.

She caught my eye. Smiled. Softly, barely, waved her hand, beckoning me.

I looked around to make sure she was gesturing to me. After all, I'd never seen her before in my life.

Yup.

She was summoning me.

I thought about it for a moment.

Ignore her, or follow her?

Maybe she recognized me?

Maybe she's the executor for a will and she's going to bequeath a fortune on me from a long-lost, filthy rich, eccentric aunt?

Or maybe she's just bat-shit crazy?

But, maybe following her might make for a good story some day?

Good enough for me. Distraction was mainly what I was after this evening. Just to get away. Get out of my headspace for a while. Hector could tell I needed it, and thankfully, offered to stay with Luis so I could just get away, just have some time to think.

It's been seven months. Most of that time I've been able to avoid thinking about it as much as possible. With a toddler and the job and marriage and everything, I've got enough on my radar to stay busy, to keep it off my mind. But he could tell I was just holding it inside. So could my counselor. They were both right. It was still on my mind. But I just kept pushing it down, only

221

letting myself break down when I was alone. Which, given my life, wasn't very often.

Tonight. In the parking lot. Here. Just before I walked in. And so, I made myself get out of the car and got inside, to the café, as quickly as I could.

And now, I was being beckoned, by this strange woman. Maybe she could read my mind? Maybe she saw me drifting too far into it, too far towards that feeling?

I gathered up my notebook and pen, picked up my coffee and walked over, tailing her deep into the bookstore.

Still silent, she led me to an enclave, back near the section where History meets Fiction. An encampment of four cushy, salmon-colored pleather chairs faced off in a large square around a dark wood table covered with discarded books and magazines.

We sat across from one another.

I put my notebook on the table, leaned forward, fingers steepled.

She looked around, then slowly leaned forward, smiled.

``You're probably wondering why I led you over here,'' she said.

``Well, yeah, the thought had crossed my mind,'' I said, with a slight chuckle.

She opened her mouth to talk, then stopped when a man dressed in a red Polo shirt and khakis wandered into our orbit. A fearful look crossed her face, she clammed up, and faded back into her chair.

I took her lead, watching the man as he browsed through the tomes for a few minutes, grabbed one and left.

She watched him go, then quickly leaned forward to me.

``Things are not as they seem,'' she said. ``I think you know that.''

``Yeah, I guess I know what you mean,'' I said.

I had no idea what she meant.

A couple sauntered around us and she hushed up again. They perused. They left. She beamed up.

``We're being watched,'' she blurted. ``They don't want you to know this.''

``Know what?'' I asked.

She smiled, leaned back. ``In time,'' she said. ``In time.''

At that point, another man, twenties, John Goodman husky build, buzz cut, sweaty, wandered through. She remained mime, giving me supposedly meaningful eye gestures and nods until he left. Once he did, she quickly resumed contact.

``I need to concentrate," she said. ``Give me a minute. I need to protect us."

She closed her eyes and breathed, long deep sighs, her hands dropped to her lap, palms up. I expected her to break into chanting. Instead she murmured a few things under her breath.

I sat there, watching her, looking around as other customers took surreptitious glances at the weirdo Martha Stewart acolyte aligning her chakras in the middle of the bookstore.

But regardless, they stayed away. No one came near. Everyone kept their distance, as if there was an invisible shield around us.

Strange, I thought.

I looked at the woman again, murmuring, eyelids flickering, looking like she was waiting to carry a cake pan I couldn't see.

Suddenly, she broke from her trance, beamed and crossed her hands on her chest.

``Okay, what did you want to know?''

``Well, first off,'' I smirked, ``what were you just doing?''

``I was . . . ''

At that moment, she was interrupted by a shambolic thirtysomething man circling around her. He looked a bit like Newman on ``Seinfeld.'' Rotund. Dark, short, shaggy haired. Pasty skin. The inklings of a mustache struggling valiantly to sprout above oddly red, I-just-drank-Kool-Aid lips. Dark, beady eyes ping-ponging behind thick, square glasses with '70s grade school class picture crap brown plastic frames.

He plopped down in the chair between the woman and me, looking around the store conspiratorially.

``See that?" he nodded to the woman and then towards a middle-aged man in Religion.

``I have the shield up," she said.

``Good," he said.

``Shield?" I asked.

``A psychic shield of protection," she said. ``That's what I was doing. Putting one up around us so we could talk with immunity."

``Immunity from what?"

``Them," the man said, pointing all around.

``Who?"

He harrumphed sardonically.

``Do you know there are cameras taping every square inch of this store?"

Okay, I have to admit it: My first thought?

Every square inch? Even the bathroom?

But instead, I said,

``Of course. They're ostensibly there to catch shoplifters."

``Ostensibly?" he said with a raised eyebrow.

``Yeah," I said. ``Ostensibly they are, and they probably do, but I used to work retail, and I know most of the security people just used the cameras to scope out hot girls and make fun of people."

``They do more than that, sweetheart," he said. ``They do more than that."

He turned to the woman, nodded slightly towards me. She smiled.

``Yes, she's clear," she said. ``She's a lightbearer. She just doesn't know it yet. They haven't made their presence known to her yet. At least not, overtly."

``What's a lightbearer?" I asked.

``You'll see when the time is right," she smiled.

"Well, isn't the time right now?"

She looked at me, and then at him, for several odd seconds as they stared at one another, making strange, subtle facial gestures.

Then she looked at me again.

"Have you ever had anything strange happen to you?"

"You mean, aside from this?"

She laughed. "I think you know what I mean."

Immediately, I knew exactly what she was talking about. Yes. Yes, I had. And it shoved its way into my head, and he was telling me to tell her, tell her about it, but as much as his voice pestered the hell out of me, as he was so, so brilliant at doing, I told him to shut up, as I was so, so brilliant, and practiced, at doing.

Instead, I decided to give her the Halloween story.

I didn't tell her about the birthday.

Or anything else.

Sorry, but I just met these people and honestly the last thing I felt like doing was going into it. I just, forget it. Fuck you, closure. Fuck you.

"I used to have this phone," I said. "It was my brother's. He used to play with it all the time when we were kids, and, uh, for some reason I ended up, it was in my parents' garage and my older brother thought it would be, he thought he'd play a joke on me or something and put it in my car and I ended up bringing it back to my house and I didn't even know I had it until I unpacked, and I just kept it around for a while.

"Anyway, this phone, it was one of those little kid phones, ya know, the kind that has the wheels on the bottom and the eyes that go up and down and the little cute smile and cheeks and it makes a funny noise and you pick it up and it has a red string that ties the receiver to the caller?"

"Yeah, I used to have one of those," the husky guy said. The older woman nodded, understanding.

"Yeah," I said, "well, from the time I brought that thing home, for some reason, my dog was just obsessed with it. The dog would follow that thing around all the time and lay by it and just kind of spend strange amounts of time looking at it. And then, one day, it started talking to me."

"Talking to you?" the man asked.

"Yeah, just out of the blue, it would blurt out random sounds. And it's not like my dog was by it, or it was set off by anything else. It was just out of the blue. I mean, sometimes it seemed like it was communicating with me or something."

"How so?"

"I don't know, it was like, I don't know. I . . . "

The woman steepled her hands and leaned towards me.

"Did you ever directly talk to it?"

I fell back in my chair a bit and actually found myself looking around. Then again, why wouldn't I tell these nutjobs? After all, how many other people have I drunkenly slurred this story to, over and over again?

"Yeah, I did," I said.

"How?"

"It started blurting out sounds one time, one time when it seemed like it was almost reading my mind or something, so I talked to it. I responded to it when it made the sounds."

"Did you call it a certain name?" the woman asked, raising an eyebrow.

Yes.

"No."

"Hmmm," she said, smiling a little. "Interesting."

"How often did you talk to it?" the man said. "Do you still talk to it?"

"No," I said. "I, stopped, it stopped talking to me."

"When did it stop talking to you?"

"I don't know, maybe a couple weeks ago."

"Interesting," the man said.

"Very interesting," the woman said.

"So, does that have anything to do with this lightbearer stuff?" I asked.

"Everything has to do with everything," the woman said, chuckling a little.

``So, is that why you chose me to invite over here out of all these people in the store?"

``That's one reason."

``What's another?"

``You were searching. You were open."

``Open to what?"

``To the knowledge."

``What knowledge?"

``See? Your curiosity only proves it," she said.

``So, what knowledge?"

She looked serenely at the man, who grumped a bit. He cleared his throat and eyeballed a thirtysomething couple who looked like they'd stepped out of the J. Crew catalogue and into our radar.

For a good five minutes my two companions were mute, volleying knowing glances to each other, punctuated by periodic nods or facial gestures as other customers sauntered through, then out of range.

``What are you guys doing?" I asked.

He rolled his eyes. She whispered.

``Communicating telepathically," she said.

``Reading minds," he said, condescendingly. ``When you have a conversation first it's all in your head. We're making sure it stays there, between us."

``Oh."

As they were doing this, I looked around at the various ``suspects" of their paranoia. Maybe one or two looked like they could possibly be involved in anything remotely close to a clandestine scheme. The rest looked like the greatest secrets they held involved how much they spent on curtains at Bed, Bath and Beyond.

``So, you're communicating telepathically, huh?" I said, once we were in the clear.

``Yes," she said.

``I'm reading your mind right now," he added, staring intently at me.

``Okay," I said, ``prove it. I'm thinking of a color. I'm thinking of everything in this department – all the books, the walls, the furniture, even your clothes, in this same color. What color is . . . "

``Orange!" he blurted.

``No."

``Red!"

``No."

``Purple."

``No."

I didn't want this to go on any further, because once you have one wrong answer it gets boring and increasingly pathetic.

``I was thinking of yellow," I said.

``Well, of course!" he said, waving his hand dismissively. ``I said orange and red, and orange is red and yellow. And she said purple, and purple is opposite yellow on the color wheel."

Of course.

``So why couldn't you just tell me yellow then?"

``Because of the mind scrambler."

``Huh?"

``The mind scrambler they have in all these stores," he said. ``They scramble your mind to cause confusion so they can better subliminally program you to want and buy certain things."

He leaned forward, excited, looked both ways, then jumped out into the figurative highway.

``See, all these places, these bookstores, are CIA secret government operations. They were set up to monitor people's intake of information, to label dissidents for when the New World Order takes over. That's why they have the cameras and all the agents milling around, to see what people are reading. And if you buy something, if you use a credit card, it's too easy. They've got your info all right there, right? All your personal information and all the books you buy are right there on the receipt, and therefore right there in their computers, and on to the master computer.

``But if you use cash, they can't get you unless they've got you on camera or under their personal surveillance.

``That's why all these huge mega-bookstores started popping up over the last decade or two. To knock off all the small bookstores, yes. The ones they can't monitor because they're owned by real patriots and independent thinkers that won't cooperate with the New World Order.

``So now they've eliminated a lot of the small, indie booksellers and they have control. But in order to utilize that control mechanism they've got to have their great monitoring apparatus in place, and they've got to be able to both watch everyone's intelligence intake and censor it by the books they choose to carry, or don't choose to carry.

``Because they're a near-monopolistic situation. They own the vast swath of the market. So if they blacklist you, if they choose not to carry your book because it has too much subversive information, then you can't get your message out and it dies on the vine."

``Yeah, but they've got a big conspiracy section over there," I said, pointing towards a large cul de sac in the back, just before the Children's section. ``It's got books on JFK, UFOs and all this New World Order stuff too. Why do they have it in the store if they're really trying to censor it?"

``They have it NOW," he said, smacking his fist against his palm. ``It's bait. To see who goes into that section, who reads or buys those books. To identify the subversives. Once the New World Order takes over, they're going to yank all of that out of here. That's when the monopoly will turn evil. And just wait until you can't get anything other than on your computer! Then they'll really have you under control and have everything under their censorship!"

He went on along the same line for a couple more paragraphs, but I found it difficult to pay attention. Once he said the line about the monopoly turning evil, all I could think of was the little rich guy on the Monopoly game cards. An evil version of him. Twisting his handlebar mustache and adjusting his monocle as he cackled over controlling Park Place, Marvin Gardens, the green state streets block and all the railroads and utilities.

When I came to again, Kool Aid Man was drifting down to earth.

``So why did you guys choose me to impart this information on?''
I asked. ``I know you think I'm curious and a lightbearer and all,
but why trust me? How did you know I wasn't one of them?''

``We've seen you here before,'' he said, leaning forward a bit and
nudging towards his female children's book companion.

``So you've been monitoring me the same way you say they
monitor you?''

``We notice things,'' she said.

``So how do I know that you're not secretly the New World
Order and you're not trying to test me or something?''

``Excellent question,'' the man said. ``You can't. But you should
ask that question. You should question everything.''

``We've seen what you've been reading,'' the woman said. "We've
even monitored what you've been writing, on your laptop. We
know that you're a traveler, seeking truth, seeking answers.
Seeking...closure."

She hung on the last word.

I hate that word.

She leaned forward.

``You just have to trust us,'' the woman added.

``Why?''

``You should trust no one," the man interjected, forcefully. ``Only yourself. Only what you know. Take our information and do with it what you will. We will be here. We know you will be here as well. We've seen you around here often enough.

``If you want to contact us, give us a sign, and we will engage you in this manner and will enlighten you further. But for now, that will have to be all. Your mind has been opened enough. We have to go."

``What? Why?"

He was looking around, seeming agitated.

``Did you see that?" he said to the woman. She nodded.

A middle-aged couple drifted over to our sector. They looked like a merlot ad. They looked like they had an altar at home dedicated to Oprah. That they probably bought from Ikea. Why were all these alleged New World Order spies people who seemed like they had once auditioned to perform in a community theater production of "The Big Chill?"

My two oddballs remained stuck in their spots, the man eyeing the new invaders to our bubble suspiciously, the woman fidgeting, then, out of the blue, looking to me.

"You know what one of my favorite books is?" she said, slyly.

"What?" I asked, expecting her to name something with the words Light, Prophecy or Ancient in the title.

"The Great Gatsby."

"Huh?"

"Have you ever read The Great Gatsby?"

"Yeah, a long time ago," I said, still a little surprised. "It's been a while."

"It's got one of the best final lines of any book," she said. "It's really a poignant ending. There's a lot of meaning, a lot of gravity, to those words."

"Okay," I said. "What are they?"

At that point, the Riunite ad couple had moved on, presumably to find something involving kittens, NASA pictures or an author they'd seen on a.m. TV interview. Or, perhaps, to get new orders from their clandestine handlers.

``We have to go," the man said.

``Wait, I didn't even get your names," I said.

``No names," he replied, tersely.

She, softer, looked at him, and then turned to me.

``I'm Cassiopeia," she said, holding out her hand. "He's Logan."

``I'm Faith," I said, shaking her hand.

``I know," she said, winking. ``I know."

"But what are the words?"

The woman took my hand one more time. "Waves don't just go out," she said, "they come back, back to the shores that are home."

She smiled, and, strange as it sounds, I felt a warmth all over, a peace, a calm, for the first time in months. I know, I know, I know, it sounds cheesy and eye-rolling and strange, but I did. I felt what I felt. I don't know why, but I did.

"Waves come back to the shores that are home."

"We have to go," Logan said, as he led Cassiopeia away towards the front of the store and the exit.

"We'll meet again," she said, hastening towards the door, before stopping for a moment and smiling. "And... congratulations."

"Congratulations? For what?"

"You'll see," she winked.

I watched them go, looked around to see if anyone followed them or spoke into a secret walkee talkee as they left, or anything like that.

Nope.

Just two people, beating a path to the door.

Hmm.

I could see them at the edge of the exit, getting ready to head into the night, and, for a second, I thought about chasing after them. It didn't matter if they were crazy or eccentric. Dead on right or full of crap. They were interesting and strange and from what I could tell, harmless, so why not hang with them a while longer, or make plans to see them again?

Why not?

I walked after them briskly, hoping to catch them just as they hit the parking lot, although oddly it seemed as if a crowd of people had decided to come in the store during that time, and I was halted before I could even get within thirty feet of the exit.

But within that time, just within a few seconds, the time it took me to weave through the throng and to the door, they disappeared.

Gone.

No sight of them anywhere.

Not in the lobby, or near the door.

Not in the parking lot.

Not in a car.

I didn't even see a car leaving the lot that could possibly be theirs. There weren't any cars leaving the lot at that time. Nothing.

I found it hard to believe that they could've vanished like that, that quickly, so I took a brief walk around the parking lot.

Nothing.

Nada.

They were gone.

And were they ever.

I never saw them there again.

Despite their assurances they would be back, they weren't.

Despite their parting words. Despite the fact they had obviously been, like me, regulars at the bookstore, judging by their comments. Despite the fact that I visited that bookstore several times a week over the next month or so.

No sign of either of them at all.

It wasn't the last time I saw them though.

Or, at least, one of them.

The woman I never saw again.

The man?

It was about a month later. I was looking through some newspapers that had accumulated on my porch. I had been busy, I had just found out, been to the doctor and knew for sure, and I thought it was time, time to clear things away, time to make a change, to move forward. A new beginning, for a new beginning.

Luis and Hector were out running errands. I was in a messy, poorly lit room, all alone but for the dog panting near my feet at the bottom of the couch. I was flipping through a newspaper from about a week or so after I'd met the pair at the bookstore.

The story was five or six pages inside, top of a page in the local news section.

A man had apparently committed suicide by jumping off Constellation Bridge.

I say apparently because reports weren't sure whether he jumped or slipped.

The name in the story wasn't Logan.

But the picture sure was.

They didn't have much information in the story about him, whatever his name was. He had a few distant relatives, but nobody had much to say. He was here. He was gone. It was sad in that it marked the passing of a human being, in a tragic way, someone I had actually met, for however short a time. It was strange. And in a way, it was somewhat chilling.

But in another way, it was somehow fitting.

After I met the couple, I told a few people about them. The reactions were mixed to say the least.

Some people think they were crazy. Those same people thought the same thing after I'd told them about the man's death. They think he was demented, suicidal and on some sort of drug or drugs. They think he obviously jumped because he was nuts, or he slipped because he was climbing on the bridge because he was nuts.

Some people chalk it up to mere coincidence and attach no significance to either event. People say weird things. People have accidents and die. It happens. The fact that it was a strange guy who held delusional thoughts was merely coincidental.

And then there are the other people.

They see a conspiracy. They think Logan knew too much. That he was pushed and it was made to look like a suicide or an accident.

I can't say I agree with them, but I do enjoy the fact they hold this opinion.

Not only because it's the most entertaining and intriguing one, the presence of which makes the world infinitely more interesting, but because, regardless of whether he was a kook or a spook, Logan would've wanted people to harbor that theory.

He would've wanted people to ascribe a special significance to his passing.

He would've relished the idea of being a catalyst for people's imaginations.

He would've been honored to have been thought of as a martyr for his cause.

Because deep down, behind that cloak of secrecy, behind his elaborate theories and ostentatious displays, I think what disturbed him most wasn't so much that people were watching him.

I think it was more about the fact that people weren't.

And he really longed, really wished, that someone had.

And so, that day, I tidied up my house, got cleaned up and dressed.

I put away my silent toy phone, packed it up in a box in the office with the rest of those things, those things, and that word, and the card from my older brother, the little postcard from my brother, and the bear, that stupid, beat up bear, and, lastly, the book.

Gatsby.

Then I walked outside, into the night, down the pathway I used to take, across the currents of traffic held static, and beyond the green light, into the unknown.

But, and it sounds strange, I finally felt fine.

I really did.

I felt fine, letting it all go. Felt fine, knowing, somehow knowing, there was going to be something, something, there.

Waves once gone to the sea, returning, to the shores they once called home.

FIFTEEN

Alex's girlfriend had discovered the body.

She was going to be watching his house and had stopped by to pick up a few things.

He was supposed to be gone.

He was.

Just not in the way she expected.

The flight had been delayed. Then canceled. Then he rescheduled. And then, according to the medical examiner, he put the phone down, went to the kitchen to get a drink, came back, sat down on the couch, turned on the TV, put down the remote, and died instantly.

He didn't even get to finish the show. Whatever it was.

His girlfriend found him, called 9-1-1, but when they got there they would tell her it was already too late. Then she called Alex's mom.

She wondered if things would've been any different. What if the flight would've been on time? Would it have changed anything? Was his being at that particular place at that particular time in any way responsible for his death?

If he had been on the plane, he would've lost a day in the time change.

The day he died might never have even existed for him.

Would that have mattered?

It seemed surreal he was gone. Simon couldn't completely make it tangible in his head. Couldn't imagine Alex as anything but vibrantly, exuberantly, full of life.

It was a massive heart attack, they said.

But he, like Simon, was only 27.

Death was something that was saved for grandparents. Creaky aunts. People he saw on holidays, who had gray hair and elephant skin and canes, who made inappropriate comments followed by craggy laughs, who mentioned old musicians named Roger and nickel movies and gross meat-based sandwich spreads and pies he'd never heard of or seen in his life.

Those were the people that died of heart attacks.

Not someone like Alex. Someone he had gone to school with since they were little kids. Someone he went to comic book shops with, played little league with, had drinking contests with on college breaks, during muggy Wisconsin summer nights near the lake after long days as camp counselors, as large groups of friends sunburned and bleached haired roamed the beaches and bars, looking for interested parties long on fun and short on reservations.

A heart attack?

A man dying that young, with no previous symptoms or history of the ailment, was unusual. Even more unusual when that man was once a champion swimmer and still made it to the gym a few times a week, even when he was living out of hotels.

Was there something more to it? Something crooked and mean? Something suspicious? Millions being gained by his convenient departure?

Or was it something airy and metaphysical? Was it just the capricious will of fate, eeney-meeney-miney-mo'ing until Alex's number came up. A tap on the chest and pop! He was gone.

It was almost too strange and incomprehensible for Simon. He felt odd that he wasn't hit harder by it, but maybe he was numb, maybe he was in denial, maybe it was too surreal at this point to even believe. He wondered if he would feel different after the funeral, after he'd seen the body, after he had no choice but to face the fact that he was really never going to see one of his oldest and closest friends alive again.

How could this be real?

It still didn't seem right, didn't seem like anything close to reality.

But it was.

On a late-night radio show, during another trek home, Simon had once heard a psychic talk about exit points. That each of us had specific times in our life that we could exit this mortal plane. We weren't aware of them, but our higher selves, our souls, were aware, and they could take the out door if they thought that we had accomplished all we were going to on this mortal plane, or if they thought we couldn't take what was to come in our lives.

Most of the time the exit points manifested themselves as accidents, freak occurrences.

A plane crash.

A skiing disaster.

A random decision veering off course.

Split seconds separated us from injury, death or a good story.

``Damn!''

Simon was jolted back to attention by a semi-trailer veering too close to his lane. Beeping manically, he pumped his brakes and let the truck pull in front of him.

``Jackass!'' He flipped the bird towards the monolith, white steel with a red diagonal band running over it.

Probably some jerk who hadn't slept in three days, guzzling truck stop speed, Simon thought.

He looked down to check his speed and noticed his gas was nearing E. Could he make it? Possibly. But why bother risking it? He knew there was an exit coming up here.

Slowly sloping into the off-ramp, he thought, maybe these were our chances to bolt, to crap out on the thunderclouds gathering in our lives, to avoid having to deal with any more heartache or pain or problems or issues or things that could help us to evolve, help us to grow as human beings, or leave us torn and tattered and damaged.

But then again, if we'd already accomplished all we needed to, if we were rolling along a plateau, then maybe that's all the time we needed.

Maybe that's what happened with Alex. After all, he'd accomplished so much, more than even he'd dreamed as a kid. Maybe his guardian angel, or whatever, thought, hey this is a perfect time to leave the party while it's still going great?

Simon stopped, parked, went into the well-lit building, did his business, meandered a few minutes around the store, picked up a couple of giant iced teas, brought them to the counter, set them down.

The visitation was tomorrow.

The funeral the next day.

And then Alex would be nothing more tangible than he was now, nothing but memories.

"Is there anything else?" the girl behind the counter looked up at Simon, sighed, seemingly annoyed.

"That's a good book," he said, perking to attention, and nodding to the dogeared paperback the girl had sitting just behind the cigarillos and beef jerky.

"Yeah," she shrugged, a little more upbeat, but still on guard.

"You reading it for class or something?"

"No, I'm just reading it because I wanted to read it."

"Really?"

"Yeah."

"Are you in school?"

"Yeah, I go to the U, I work here part time, and I like to read for fun. Is there anything else?"

"No, no, just the caffeine."

They exchanged money, she looked down, he walked out.

Taking a deep drink as he returned to his car, he noticed the last line of light -- dark pink and purple on the horizon. The sun had disappeared, the blues of the sky darkened in front of him, distilling from indigo and cobalt as they smudged away from the pastels of the west. The first stars became visible in the rich eastern navy.

He pushed on the gas and his clunky Toyota valiantly shouldered through the gears, getting back up to 65 and onto the highway, breezing past another green-and-white sign informing the journey ahead, detailing the next three exit points.

Exit points.

Dozens of them along the way.

And at one of them, a funeral for a friend.

Who had, perhaps, finally decided to take one his own.

He thought back for a second to the girl in the shop.

On the way to the car, Simon's first reaction was that the girl was incredibly rude and he was just trying to make conversation, curious about the book. His second reaction was that she was probably used to a bunch of jerks just like him trying to hit on her, she was sick of it, and the best way she found to get rid of them was to cut them short. His third reaction was disappointment that people had to be that way in the first place, and that if the guys who'd gone in there hadn't been such assholes, she wouldn't have changed and developed that thick skin.

But then by the time he got to the car, he realized he'd developed an entire narrative for the girl and what had just happened, and it was based entirely upon his own assumptions, which had just as much a chance of being wrong as her assumptions that he was just a moron looking to make lewd comments to her or pick her up, instead of just making casual conversation.

But then again, maybe, just maybe, if his own mind wasn't so preoccupied with other things, he wouldn't have been seeking this distraction to even give much thought to it? He would've walked in, paid for his stuff, seen the book and said nothing, and just walked out, because in his mind he would've thought 'oh, interesting, but I really don't feel like talking' and he would've completely forgotten about it by the time he got to the car.

But the fact was, it didn't really matter much either way.

The end result was the same. He went in, got something, paid for it, and left. That was their interaction. Anything else, anything either of them thought of each other, good or bad, was completely within their own minds.

He thought about this again a couple days later, when he was on the same highway, headed back home.

The funeral had been just as bad as he'd dreaded. It had brought the situation to a striking finality and a crushingly depressing reality, and he didn't feel much like thinking about it, and was searching for pretty much anything to take his mind off it.

Unsuccessfully.

He thought of the night before the funeral, what it was like to spend the night in his old room at his parents' house, and how different it was, how small it seemed now.

For a while, from the time they bought it, when he was just a kid, to the time he moved out, when he went to college, it was the center of his universe, where he'd go to listen to music and read and do homework and play video games and hang out with his friends and read books and call the girls he'd had relationships with as a teen.

He thought of those girls, and the few that he'd seen at the funeral. It was like a high school reunion. All of these people who hadn't seen each other in years, and yet they were all frozen in time to each other, their feelings for one another exactly the same as those which they'd had when they'd last seen each other in person, five, ten years before.

And yet they were, in many ways, different people. Not just in that way that every seven years the cells of your body are supposed to regenerate and that you're literally a new person (which Simon often thought was kind of dubious and wondered how he could possibly control that, and alter his cells enough to get him to be better looking or in better shape), but in their personalities, the people they were.

They'd been through things -- marriages, kids, one or two even a divorce already. That had to change them, somehow, the same way Simon had changed, the same way Alex wasn't the same person he'd been.

And yet all their memories, all the things they'd talked about, were from so long ago, back when Alex was a different person. Back before he was successful. Back before he was confident. Back before he had done any of the things he had done.

Back when he and Simon had so much more, really, in common.

And yet it was that time, that short, short, era of just a couple of years, that defined Alex more than any on this, the last formal day of his life, so to speak. His body's final farewell, at least.

There they were, all the pallbearers, aside from his brother, were friends he hadn't seen in years, people who were such a huge part of his life when he was a teenager, before he'd left, before he'd moved out, and back when his parents saw him the most. Maybe that's why his parents considered that the most important era, and those people the most important friends, when they chose his pallbearers and the people who would stand by him, one last time.

They wanted to recapture that again.

Not just his life, but that point in his life, that point when they'd seen him the most, when he was still their child, still this being they could look at and remember when he was little, when he was three, six, nine, a baby.

Alive.

Alive, and with all that future, all that time ahead of him, and all that certainty they had that he would be there with them.

In the audience was his girlfriend, the one who'd found his body, the one who'd seen him alive the last time, who had loved him, who had maybe known him better than anyone currently. And along with her were dozens of other people, other friends, who had never known him as a teen. Who had seen him far more frequently than Simon had in the past several years.

And yet, Simon thought, there he was at the front, one of the people who saw Alex's dead face last, who lowered him down into the earth. The last image he, and anyone, would all have of him. Their years, their friendships, their time with him, was what was chosen to define them as his closest friends, to define him, as theirs.

Landing on Mars.

They were the spot considered to be the best chance at finding any remaining life, or memory of it, for those so desperately wanting to find it.

And Simon thought about all the people Alex had met in the last seven years or so that maybe hadn't talked to Alex in a while, who maybe hadn't heard he'd died.

They were still out there. Oblivious.

To them, he was still alive, still a living being, still a possibility. Not just a memory, not someone being mourned and contemplated, but someone far breezier, someone they were going to call, going to get together with, going to hang out with again soon, soon, once they got back to Cali or Alex made his way through to them.

They had no idea. No idea he'd died.

They were still in orbit.

Exit points taken in and out of each other's lives. We touch down, for a short time, see what we see, see what we want to see, filtered through our eyes, and then we take off, with an image, a perception, of a world that exists only in our mind, based on our limited experience.

When all we're seeing is a tiny bit. Whether it's through the limited scope of our eyes, or through a glass, a telescope. All of them just catching a tiny fraction, a limited spectrum, of a massive universe of being, a vast expanse of experience and humanity, that's constantly moving, constantly evolving.

Constantly changing, constantly turning, constantly returning.

Exit points.

And landing points.

An infinite galaxy of them around us, and living within us.

All as we focus on finding life on Mars.

But only life as we know it.

Maybe not life as it really is.

Waves, infinite space, galaxies, moving at the speed of light, the speed of our thoughts, the speed of our dreams.

Waves, carried out into that unfathomable ocean of energy and imagination, but sometimes, sometimes, finding their way back to the place they once called home.

SIXTEEN

"I love you."

He looked into the face of his new son.

Eyes clear and blue.

He held him close, as his father had held him, so many years before.

As he had held his father, not so long ago.

"I love you."

The baby's mother, exhausted, slept, as the tiny boy snuggled warm in the arms of his father.

The man had never needed much sleep, and now, buzzed on adrenaline from the rush of his son's birth just a few hours earlier, he settled into a large chair, pulled tight to his wife's bed, close by her, and held their son, close to his chest, close to his heart.

He nuzzled his nose against the baby's, slowly, as the boy's serene, soft wrinkled face peeked out from a cozy, blue blanket, large and secure around them.

Like a big nest.

And the new father held him, his baby, like his father had held him when he was a child, and like he had held his own father not so long ago.

He looked into his blue, blue eyes.

His face.

His little nose.

His wispy hair.

His chubby cheeks.

His pokey ears.

His lips, slightly curved as if about to smile.

And his blue, blue eyes.

He looked so much like him.

And, like him.

His baby bird.

"Tweet tweet," he whispered.

"Tweet tweet."

And the baby's eyes opened wider, wider, until the man felt a strange current wash over him, warm and peaceful, fluttering in his heart.

"Love you baby bird," he whispered.

The boy's tiny fingers began to move like waves rolling onto the ocean beach on a summer morning.

"Love you."

Slowly, tenderly, the baby reached out and touched the man's hand.

"Love you, baby bird."

Tiny fingers, fragile and fine, grasped the older man's hand, holding it, tentative at first, and then, tighter.

"I love you."

The baby's watery eyes closed, and his little lips seemed to smile, and then, his eyes broke open slowly, letting the black curtains part and the sleeves of light, pure and white, reach in, filling his mind with wonder.

Before him was the face of his father, tears in his eyes, looking down into parallel pools of brilliant blue.

He held him in his arms, close to his heart, as his father had once done for him.

"Tweet tweet, baby bird," he said. "Tweet tweet."

And the baby's blue eyes grew wide and he smiled a little smile, safe, serene, happy, and he reached out again to hold his hand, gently, steadfastly, close by his father's heart.

The man looked at the new life before him, taking his first breaths, so much like the old life he'd held as he breathed his last. He felt his heart, beating strongly, vibrantly, close to his own, as they snuggled, tucked into a large blanket, enveloping and warm around them, like a nest.

Like...home.

"Love you baby bird," the man said, through tears.

And Finn Barstow looked into the eyes of his son, Nick, named after his father he loved so much, who he missed so much. Who once held Finn, so small, close to his heart.

He looked into his eyes, and he saw a universe. And Nick looked back into Finn's eyes, and he saw home.

"Love you, baby bird."

Looked into his eyes and saw his universe.

"Love you, Daddy bird."

Reborn.

"I love you."

Thank you for taking this journey.

Other Books By Sean Leary

The Arimathean (novel)

The Blood of Destiny (novel)

Black Knight Apocalypse (novel)

The Arimathean Files (non-fiction)

Luna Death Trigger (novel)

DisIntegration (novel)

Does The Shed Skin Know It Was Once A Snake? (short stories)

Every Number Is Lucky To Someone

(short stories)

My Life As A Freak Magnet

(short stories)

Exorcising Ghosts

(graphic novel)

Here Comes The Goot!

(children's/beginning readers)

Go, Racecars, Go!

(children's/beginning readers)

Nine Little Penguin Ninjas

(children's/beginning readers)

Baby Bird

(children's/beginning readers)

We Are All Characters

(children's/beginning readers)

Beautiful Remnants of Chaotic Failures

(poetry)

Danger Maps

(poetry)

Every Broken Heart Creates The Pieces That Will Pave The Way To The Place Your Heart Will Call Home

(poetry)

Tricks of the Light

(poetry)

The Soft Venom of Promise

(poetry)

The Night Universal

(poetry)

There Is Truth In The Untamed Beat of a Heart

(poetry)

We Are Shadows In The Absence of Light

(poetry)

Magnets & Mysteries, Soft Curves & Comets

(poetry)

Infinite Sky

(poetry)

Physics & Beauty

(poetry)

Dark Equinox

(graphic novel)

The Ink In The Well

(graphic novel)

Dream States

(graphic novel)

Valentine Cords

(graphic novel)

Spyder

(graphic novel)

Sean Leary's Greatest Hits, volume one

(humor)

Sean Leary's Greatest Hits, volume two

(humor)

Sean Leary's Greatest Hits, volume three

(humor)

Sean Leary's Greatest Hits, volume four

(humor)

Sean Leary's Greatest Hits, volume five

(humor)

Sean Leary's Greatest Hits, volume six

(humor)

Sean Leary's Greatest Hits, volume seven

(humor)

Your Favorite Band

(stageplay / screenplay)

Dingo Boogaloo

(stageplay / screenplay)

Rock City Live!

(stageplay / screenplay)

My Life As A Freak Magnet: The Scripts

(stageplay / screenplay)

Shots To The Heart, volumes one and two

(stageplays)

Advice to My Son

(life stories and positive parenting)

Do Vampires Poop?

(humor)

The Devil Shops At Target

(humor)

I Don't Have The Map

(poetry)

For more see

www.seanleary.com.

www.ingramcontent.com/pod-product-compliance
Lightning Source LLC
Chambersburg PA
CBHW020614260626
47157CB00003B/1006